The Devil's Soul

Book 3 of the Sister Witches

FELICIA JEDLICKA

Felicia Jedlicka
Find me on Facebook: www.facebook.com/feljedauthor
Visit my website feljedauthor.wordpress.com

For those willing to start over; even if that means leaving a part of yourself behind.

More titles by FELICIA JEDLICKA

DESTINY REJECTED
DESTINY RECLAIMED
DESTINY RAZED
DESTINY RESTORED

DÉJÀ VU

SAVE THE HUMANS

THE NECROMANCER'S CHILD

SISTER WITCHES
THE DEVIL'S SHADOW
THE DEVIL'S SOUL

THE NEBRASKA APOCALYPSE NOVELS
CORN COWS AND THE APOCALYPSE
COW TIPPING AFTER THE APOCALYPSE
CORN HUSKING AFTER THE APOCALYPSE

THE WARDEN SERIES
SUCCESSORS
RIVALS
LOVERS AND LIARS
BAD BLOOD
TENANTS AND TYRANTS
THE RING BEARER
GODS AND MONSTERS
BEASTS AND BURDENS
MAGIC AND MAYHEM
FORK IN THE ROAD
DETAILS AND DEADLINES

The Devil's Soul

Book 3 of the Sister Witches

FELICIA JEDLICKA

PROLOGUE

I NEVER MEANT TO become the villain.

All I ever wanted was a normal life, with family and friends to share it with. Maybe a husband and children.

Is that really why I left hell? Why I broke from the devil and possessed this body? Did Satan's soul want to live as a human, experience love, joy, and contentment? I must have. That's the only explanation for why I feel so empty now.

Well, not empty. I still have Hennie—the original Hennie. With the help of the beast, whom she stupidly invited into her, she has been slogging her way to the surface. Quite literally clawing her way out of me. However, there is nowhere to go. All she really wants is to die and if she gets control of this body again, she might do just that.

It's true I had permission to be in this body. God Himself said so. Or rather, God told my former coven member, Rachel, and then she told me. But, of course, she doesn't remember telling me, so she and the rest of the coven still think I am an incarnation of evil and want to pull my soul from this body and send it back to hell where it belongs.

In fact, they are so determined to remove me they teamed up with one of hell's trinity to do so. Paula, or Paul in her manly form, is a free-form walking, talking version of the devil. She used to be a member of our coven and the convent we used as a cover for our work. Despite revealing her true identity, she still appears to me as a nun. A rather confusing persona, since I'd cared for her a good deal when she was pretending to be a diplomatic edifier. But that was the point. The ram was always a master manipulator—turning even our deepest beliefs against us as a weapon.

As if it wasn't bad enough that my former coven had teamed up with the devil to kill me, my boyfriend—or I guess he was now my ex-boyfriend—had also turned against me. It's hard to explain his motivations for this. He was a serial killer of women before the coven interned him. With the help of some powerful magic, we cleaned his soul, burdened him with guilt, and granted him the ability to see and touch demons. His duty to the coven was to protect us from the dangers we couldn't see. Though Dane had never disguised his predatory draw to me, I had always assumed it would remain carnal. It didn't.

That's why I found myself hitchhiking across the country, jumping from job to job, and staying in cheap motels. Because if I stopped for too long, or used my power, he would find me, and the coven would follow and kill me.

Chapter 1

"Hey!" a man in a flannel shirt and baseball cap called over to me. "You gonna bring that coffee to me or just model it?"

I snapped out of my reverie to stare at the customer. For a moment, I'd forgotten why he was there or why I was there, or why any of us were here. It was a frequent occurrence since my former self—the original Hennie—had surfaced. It was as if she would take over my brain for a moment. However, since she had been brain-dead and in a coma when I'd possessed her, she wasn't exactly the best driver for this vehicle.

I forced the movement back into my body with a gentle mental nudge to its previous occupant. I put on a fake smile and walked over to the booth I was meant to be serving. Working as a truck stop waitress had to be on my list of top ten worst jobs. Granted, I had no college degree, no formal training of any kind, and my work history consisted of two fast-food restaurants I'd worked at while I was in high school, but somehow I thought I deserved better.

My somewhat deserved ego might have come from the fact that I had access to a rather dangerous level of power. Or maybe I felt being the first soul ever created put me a touch higher on the food chain than the average human. Then again, it could have also been because I had more teeth than most of the people I was serving.

Naturally, my feelings of superiority had to be suppressed. I couldn't use my power and risk alerting Dane to my location. Plus, I would probably just end up killing someone—and despite what my coven might think, I am not evil. Also, I had to behave because I needed the tips. My hotels might be cheap, but they weren't free.

"Sorry about that. I had a brain injury when I was young and I can't always stay focused," I told the man as I poured coffee into his travel mug. It wasn't really a lie, and I was hoping my honesty about my condition would inspire pity and a higher tip.

"You must have been hit pretty hard," he grumbled as he pulled out his wallet.

I set down the coffee and ripped the check off my pad. He looked over the amount and frowned. I was hoping he would complain about the cost of breakfast. That was my absolute favorite to listen to while I was working for $2 an hour and begging for tips like a flat-chested stripper. Fortunately, he kept his complaint to himself, but obviously took his anger out on my portion of the tip. My day was rounding up to $3 an hour. Hooray for capitalism!

He slapped the bills on the check and slid it over to me. "I guess a half-brained waitress gets half the—Jesus!" His eyes went wide as he looked at something on me. "What the hell are you doing to yourself?"

I looked down at where he was staring. My right hand was viciously scratching my left forearm. I couldn't feel the bleeding cuts, nor was I aware my hand was doing it. Hennie.

I forced myself back into control and grabbed a napkin from the dispenser on the table. I pressed it over the blood as a temporary bandage. "I'm sorry, I have..." I searched through my Rolodex of excuses: it's a mosquito bite from hell, a rash, leprosy, schizophrenia?

He didn't give me a chance to express my excuse. "Listen, honey, do yourself a favor." He scooted out of the booth. "Either get off the drugs or back on them, cause you're useless right now."

Before he could slip past me, I rested my hand on his shoulder. "You have a good day, sir."

The man's eyes glazed as I put a spoonful of magic into my touch. "Yeah, you too." He reached for his wallet and flipped through the bills until he reached the hundreds. He pinched three of them as if they were one-dollar bills and tossed them on the table with his other money. "Hope you brought an umbrella. Looks like the clouds are rollin' in." He stood and walked away, none the wiser to my magical influence.

It was dangerous to play with it in this way, but I really needed to pay my hotel bill and a little magic wasn't likely to broadcast like a beacon. Just a blip. I would move on eventually, anyway.

I looked out at the clouds the trucker had commented on. They really were rolling in. I was now convinced my presence actually brought bad weather. Even out here in the desert, outside of monsoon season, I could summon tears from a dry sky.

I grabbed the hundreds and folded them tight. I looked back to see if Doris noticed me keeping such a large tip, but she was busy with her customers at the counter. She always worked at the counter. It was her prerogative since she owned the place, but it meant I had to run my ass off around the restaurant, while her fat ass had everything within arm's reach. Not that she didn't complain about it, anyway.

As I slipped my tip into my bra, I noticed a man in the corner booth watching me. I assumed any motion that put my hands near my chest intrigued him, but he didn't readily avert his eyes when I caught him watching. Much like the other men frequenting this establishment, he wore jeans, a plaid shirt, and a dirty baseball cap that glorified a sports team or company product.

However, unlike the usual clientele, he was not blooming a beer belly from excess pancake consumption. He was young, so there was still time, but something told me the potential six-pack under his button-down shirt was not likely to disappear any time soon.

Besides his outstanding physique, he was attractive. There was no guarantee if the brown hair curling from under his cap covered his entire head, but his chin was definitely bald. His clean-shaven face had a boyish appeal that contrasted with Dane's more robust features. I wasn't sure if I preferred this man's more angular face, but six months without companionship was leaving me with cravings that chocolate and wine couldn't satisfy.

I gave the man a demure smile, and he gave me a cocksure grin. I moved over to his table and leaned against it. I found his choice of the corner booth extremely obnoxious since he was only one person, but I let it go. "What can I get you?" I asked with a slight hint of seduction.

I wasn't sure if I could pull off seductive in my waitress uniform. The turquoise dress was tight, and the skirt was short. However, I wasn't sure the grease and ketchup stains screamed sexy. My sloppy bun left the black tips of my white-blond hair flaring out like a boring peacock's tail. My nose ring was the only jewelry I wore, along with my tiny cross necklace which I kept beneath my collar, touching my skin at all times. It was my litmus test for evil.

"How about a date?" he asked boldly. I liked that. I wasn't in the mood for games.

"I get off at seven," I answered just as boldly. His smile grew into a mischievous grin. He apparently wanted to skip the games as well. "Are you staying at the motel?" I nodded in the general direction of my temporary home.

"How about I meet you back here?" he suggested.

"Don't you want me to change into something nicer?"

He puckered his lips and shook his head. "No, I really don't." The way he said it made me think he had a fetish for costumes. However, I really didn't care. I wanted what he was offering and likewise. If I had better stamina for stand-up sex, I would have proposed a meeting in the bathroom in five minutes.

"Okay, see you then." I walked away, but turned back. "I'm sorry, did you want food too?"

He chuckled and shook his head. "No." He nodded to my arm. "You might want to get that covered up."

I looked down and caught myself scratching the same spot again. I had drawn more blood. I clenched my jaw, internally screaming at Hennie to knock it off. I put back on a fake smile and walked away before he could change his mind about meeting up later.

"Hennie!" Doris scolded me as I walked by the counter to get to the kitchen. "What have I told you about using the Brillo pad on these napkin dispensers?" She held up one of her dispensers. The silver should have been a shiny chrome, but I had scrubbed it so hard all the sheen was gone. It now looked like brushed silver instead of polished silver.

I shrugged at her. "Sorry, the syrup just wouldn't come off."

"I swear, you are almost not worth the trouble," she grumbled as she wobbled over to grab her next order.

"Neither are you," I said under my breath and pushed through the doors to the kitchen.

"Don't let her get to you, Hennie," Mateo, the cook, said as I walked past his griddle station. "You're doing fine."

Although I appreciated his compliment, I knew he was only trying to earn some points with me. He would have said or done most anything to get an invitation to my hotel room. But unlike the man who just did, Mateo was in his forties, married with two kids, and covered with enough body hair to qualify him as a werewolf. I was certainly desperate for some manly attention, but I was not about to get tangled up in *that* mess—literally or figuratively.

"Thanks, Mateo." I gave him a wave and headed over to the emergency eyewash station. I opened the medicine cabinet hanging above it and pulled out a roll of gauze. I wrapped the fabric around my wound as thickly as I could to keep my nails from digging into it again. I tucked the fabric in on itself and closed the cabinet.

I nearly shrieked at the sight of the black-haired, handsome man behind me. Though his features were that of Paul—the male version of Paula—this was technically a different member of hell's trinity. While the beast was a manifestation of hatred used to torment humans, and the ram was a physical presence designed to infiltrate humanity and corrupt it from within, the serpent, aka my shadow, was the seducer. For all intents and purposes, he was the brains of the operation and the owner of my soul.

He had pushed his morality aside time and time again in order to do the evil deeds that the devil must do. Since he had already split himself into three parts—mind, body, and raging temper—it wasn't unheard of for his last remaining shred of goodness to become sentient and run away.

As he constantly reminded me, though, I couldn't truly get away from him. We were effectively the same being. I could only see him through a reflection and we couldn't touch. However, I sensed him when he was near. My connection to the hellish power he gave me was addictive.

But, as a former junkie and not a current junkie, I no longer used his power. I wasn't supposed to use *any* magic, but when I did, I sneaked it directly from my origin of creation. My soul. The devil's soul. The fact that he had fallen from grace and bathed in hellfire didn't change the fact that God had designed the soul for an angel. The magic I got from it was clean and empowering in a way that made me believe I was the most powerful being on Earth.

And since that belief was actually true, I used it as infrequently and as delicately as possible. The last thing I needed to do was throw god-level powers around every time Doris told me to plunge the toilet. I had to be a good little human and not turn her into a pile of ash. Even though I could, I wouldn't.

But I could.

"What do you want?" I whispered to keep my split personality conversation away from eavesdroppers.

My shadow looked me over. He was no doubt disappointed by my attire. While he was in his dapper suit and tie with a perfectly trimmed mustache and goatee, I was a stain-covered waitress. "Why are you doing this to yourself?"

"Because I need money," I answered.

"You can summon enough power to mark the beginning of the apocalypse. Why would you demean yourself to work in the food industry?"

"Because I like smelling like grease. Can we skip the lectures and get to the update?"

He grimaced and nodded. "Dane has now rejoined the coven. They are combining their efforts to find you. It won't be long before your masking spells fail. Dane is proving to be quite a formidable hunter." I ignored the ache in my heart. I had already broken it. What was one more fracture?

"What about Paula?"

"She is still assisting them as needed, but they are reluctant to use her power."

"And if Rachel agrees to combine them?"

"Rachel and Paula's combined power will likely be enough to remove you from this body. Though not without a hell of a fight."

"And that's what they'll get because I'm not giving up this life. I don't know why, but God wants me here."

My shadow chuckled and rested his chin on my shoulder. I felt the tingle of his presence, but it was more internal than external. "Poor little Hennie, you're just an experiment to him and a lesson for me. He doesn't really care about you."

Before I could stop my reaction, my power surged and the mirror shattered. I frowned at the broken pieces in the sink. "Doris," I called in a sing-song voice. "The cabinet mirror broke... again."

CHAPTER 2

S EVEN O'CLOCK WAS TAKING its sweet-ass time arriving. As I stared out the front windows of the diner, I wondered if I could fast-forward time. Surely that was a God-only sort of power. But, perhaps, I could nullify my consciousness of it. Then again, the more I thought about it, the more I realized it would be a self-limiting endeavor.

Something caught my eye as I turned back to roll my silverware. A shadow. A wispy blob of pure evil came around the corner of the building outside. It disappeared, and then two more appeared.

Demons.

Since my transition to using my internal power source, I had somehow unlocked my ability to see the wily little bastards. Not that it did me any good. I still couldn't touch them. And with an ixnay on all power usage, I couldn't even scare them away. The only good thing about them was I had an early warning system for trouble.

In the last waitress job I'd worked, a trio of demons had come into the cafe in search of trouble. They'd settled on a couple of guys who'd turned out to be planning a robbery. While they patiently waited for the place to quiet down, I monitored the demons, sniffing them like rabid dogs. It wasn't until the guns were up in the air and people started screaming that I'd understood their intent.

I should have given them the money. I should have cowered behind the counter and played the victim. But, of course, I had to mouth off to them. I would like to say it was my more recent stressors that had caused me to behave so flippantly, but my belligerence started long ago on school playgrounds. I had a knack for pissing people off.

My baiting words resulted in a knife being pressed to my throat, as if his partner's gun in my face wasn't threatening enough. Rather than get angry or pick a fight my human body wasn't capable of winning, I tapped the powder keg inside of me.

It was just a little, I promise, but, oh, how theatrical I was. My shadow was proud of me that day.

"Bleed," I said with a resonant voice.

At first, the men didn't understand the threat I posed to them. When blood started to drip from their eyes, ears, and noses, they became alarmed. They dabbed at it, wiped it away, each gawking at the other with a horror-stricken expression.

"Break." The word was out of my mouth before I could comprehend what the result would be.

Break, they did. Every bone in their bodies snapped like twigs. The audible sound sent chills through me and further terrified the hostages in the cafe.

It wasn't until I saw the men lying on the ground crying like babies and pleading for God's help that I recovered from my momentary ego trip and lapse of judgment. Guilt flooded me as I looked around at the patrons, who were no longer afraid of guns and knives. It was the strange waitress in the center of the room that caused their flinching. I could even smell the urine of someone who was so distressed they lost control of their bladder.

This was not what heroes did. This was what sick sadistic freaks did.

I summoned my power one last time, going well beyond what I ever had.

"Heal," I said, and the men stopped screaming. "Forget," I said, and the patrons stopped whimpering. "Resume," I said and jumped to the men on the floor.

"Oh, my God, I'm sorry. I should have put a wet floor sign out." I carried on, explaining my stupidity even as the men tried to fathom why they were on the floor, covered in blood. They each tucked away their weapons and exchanged baffled looks. I pleaded for my job and begged them not to sue the cafe. Naturally, the men left as quickly as possible without further trouble. A moment later, another man scurried from his table and left the building. I didn't bother chasing him down for the check. He had more pressing concerns.

I didn't even finish my shift that day. My power usage was a beacon to my *enemies*. I had no choice but to flee my new home again. A month here. A few weeks there. Who was I kidding? I no longer had homes. I had hideouts and safe houses.

My efforts to maintain a normal life had failed so many times I no longer held any hope for it. Now I just wanted some measure of peace. No more fighting. No more...

Trouble.

I watched three, then four, then six demons flutter and float around the corner of the building. They weren't sniffing out danger, as I had assumed. They had already found it.

Emerging from the horde of do-no-goods was a man. Six feet tall, broad shoulders, and enough muscle to reconsider a fight with. For a half-second, I thought it was Dane, but the scraggly brown beard and over-sized nose definitely didn't belong to him.

The man adjusted the crotch of his pants before he reached for the door. The bells jingled as he entered. He stood there a moment, looking over the nearly vacant restaurant. The only other customer was Lyle—a regular who came in for dinner every night around the same time. With few exceptions, he was the only person I looked forward to seeing every day. He was an older man with kind eyes. His manners were admirable for an establishment like this one, and he always left me a ten-dollar tip no matter what he ordered. Sometimes he even let me pick his order since I knew better than him what was safe to eat in this place and what wasn't. With him as a potential victim to any fight I might pick with this asshole, I was certain my guns would stay holstered.

"Well, howdy there, sweetheart," the trucker said to me as he moved over to the counter. "Where do I sit to get your service?" Though he said it with humor in his voice, the demons swirling around him made it sound lewder.

"I'm the only one here, so you can sit anywhere."

He perked a brow as he sat at the counter. "The only one here?" he asked. The smile on his face turned to a smirk and the darkness of the demons merged behind him, making it look as if his very aura had darkened.

"Well, besides the cook." I turned to the window and shouted through it, "Hey, Mateo, say hello."

After a moment, Mateo popped into view. He wasn't especially tall, and he was more burly than muscled, but it didn't matter. The effect of his presence came more from the eight-inch cleaver in his hand. He held it high for the man to see—a routine Doris had implemented long before I arrived. She may have been lazy, but she wasn't stupid. She knew that roadside traffic was a mixed bag, and she wasn't about to have her staff harassed.

"Hi," Mateo said with a flat expression.

"Howdy," the trucker said.

"I'm just bustin' some chops back here, Hennie. You give a holler when you need me." Mateo looked at the man. "I'll hear you," he said and disappeared into the kitchen again.

The trucker chuckled and nodded. "Good guy."

"Yes, he is," I said. "He's also an excellent cook. What can I get you?" I pulled out my pad and took down his order. I slipped it into the rotary and poured him a fresh cup of coffee. I tried to tempt him with a piece of pie, as Doris demanded I do, but he claimed not to be a dessert kind of guy. As if he wasn't evil enough already.

When his food arrived on the sill, I brought it over and let him take his first bite before asking how he liked it. He groaned with enjoyment and declared it the best chicken fried steak he had ever had. I thanked him on behalf of Mateo and searched my pockets for something. I pulled out a smashed soft pack of cigarettes that only contained two cancer-sticks and leaned over the counter to whisper to him.

"Hey, I'm just dying for a smoke. If Mateo asks for me, say I went to the restroom, would ya?"

"Sure thing," he said with a conspiratorial wink.

As I headed to the door, I asked Lyle if he needed anything. He gave me a small smile and shook his head. He wasn't much of a talker, which was another reason I liked him.

I slipped out the door, careful not to agitate the bells, which would signal my impromptu *smoke* break to Mateo. I didn't actually smoke. The pack had fallen out of someone's pocket in the bathroom. I started using them as an excuse to get an extra break or two. Since Doris was a heavy smoker herself, she couldn't argue with the logic.

The setting sun had colored the sky a perfect shade of pink, making the red desert dirt glow. It was a beautiful sight, one I no longer took for granted. At some point in my travels, I had lost focus on why I was running. It wasn't just to live, but to experience *life*. I wasn't sure what hell was like, but I knew I wouldn't see sunsets there. It was cliché to say that every day was a gift, but for me, it was. I didn't have the luxury of looking forward to reincarnation or heaven. My death would result in a one-way ticket back to hell where I would rejoin my shadow and effectively no longer exist. Death, for me, was the absolute end.

I waited for the colors in the sky to shift into more muted tones of orange before I unlocked my gaze and headed back into the dinner. However, my eyes found an unfamiliar sight to gawk at when I turned around.

The parking lot around the diner was rather extensive since it shared real estate with a gas station, a hotel, and a small laundromat. With most of the clientele being truckers, they needed ample room to park their rigs. There was a cluster of six trucks parked alongside the diner, one of which I was sure belonged to the man inside.

My mouth gaped as I stared at the vortex of darkness above one of the semi-trailers. More than a dozen demons were swimming in the negative energy being produced by it. Unlike the danger-seeking demons that had latched onto the driver, suffering lured these parasites in. I was certain I would find multiple victims in the back of that truck.

"So much for keeping a low profile," I mumbled to myself.

CHAPTER 3

B ACK INSIDE THE DINER, I stared at the truck driver, trying to discern what kind of monster he was. Was he a killer? Was he a sex trafficker? A child molester? Or did he just kick puppies and spit on babies? My instincts told me he was one of those things.

Truthfully, it didn't matter what his crime was. The only important question cycling through my head was: *Should I do something about it*? I could call the police, but with very little to go on, what do I say? I met a trucker who may or may not be doing something bad?

No, my options were the same as they had always been: use my power to be the hero and call in a team of highly talented witches to kick my ass straight down to hell... or do nothing and *deserve* to be kicked straight down to hell.

As a normal human, I could blame my lack of action on ignorance and fear, but I had neither. I knew something terrible was going on in the back of that semi-trailer and I had to find out what it was and put a stop to it. Even if it meant exposing myself.

Damn you, conscience.

"So," I drawled and leaned over the counter. Despite my collar being too high to see any cleavage, the trucker still tried to look down my shirt. "You here for a pit stop, or are you tuckin' in for the night?"

He smiled and perked his brow suggestively. "Why, you lookin' for some overnight company?" I restrained a laugh. Even if he wasn't dripping with evil, I had no interest in him. Aside from his enormous nose turning me off, he seemed to have no concept of how to chew with his mouth closed. Why did people think that was an option? "What's your name?"

"Hennie. You?"

"Pete."

"What's your number, Pete?" I nodded toward the hotel.

He smiled and rolled his tongue around, collecting the last of his bite lodged between his teeth. Seriously, food in; close mouth! How hard is that? "Number 6."

Of course it was.

"Must be my lucky number," he said.

"We'll see. These late nights wear me out."

"You don't have to lift a finger, darling," he purred.

I probably looked drawn in by his flirtation, seconds from jumping his bones right there on the counter. However, the sinister look in my eyes was because I wanted to cut his tongue out. And not even metaphorically, I had already plotted out the steps it would take to grab the steak knife off his napkin, wrench open his jaw, and lasso his tongue. And once again, I could do it... but I wouldn't. Not until I found out what kind of bad guy he was.

With thoughts of my legs wrapped around him later, Pete hurried through his last bites and paid his bill so he could go shower before our "date." The minute he left, and the bells stopped ringing, I gagged and made a sour face.

I looked over at Lyle, suddenly remembering he was still at his booth. He was looking at me with a worried expression. Not so much, I assumed, because of my sound effects, but because a young woman making advances on an older man was likely to send his grandfatherly instincts into overdrive. "Don't worry, Lyle. I'm not going." I grabbed the coffee off the warmer and headed over to his booth.

He watched me refill his cup and then gave me a small smile that reminded me of a newborn baby trying to make the muscles of the mouth work. I smiled back at him and tipped my head to one side. "You don't talk much, do you?"

He shrugged. "Don't have much to say."

"Oh, I bet that's not true. I bet you have lots of stories." I sat down in the booth across from him, even though he hadn't invited me. I set down the coffee and folding my arms on the table. "Can I ask you a question?"

"Okay."

"Why do you come in here every night? The food isn't *that* good."

"Hey!" Mateo scolded me from the counter. I hadn't noticed he had come out to grab Pete's dishes—something *I* should be doing. I laughed at him and waved him away.

Lyle averted his eyes and cleared his throat, which caused a brief bout of coughing. He wiped his mouth with his napkin and I noticed a small amount of blood on it when he pulled it away. My heart ached at the thought of what ailment he might have.

"My wife and I used to come here every Sunday for our evening meal. It was her rule, you see. She was an excellent housekeeper and a fine cook, but she said that even God gets to have one day off a week." Lyle let out a breathy chuckle. "So, on Sunday mornings, we ate cold cereal before church. For lunch, we microwaved canned soup. And for supper, we went out to eat. She didn't cook or clean all day. That was her rule."

I smiled. "That's a great rule." I pinched back my lips, not wanting to ask the next question. "How did you lose her?"

Lyle opened his mouth, considering his words. "She was having a headache, and she went into the bedroom to lie down. When I came to check on her later, she had already passed."

Tears welled in my eyes, but I noticed Lyle wasn't nearly as distraught by the conversation as I was. He had either already cried enough for her or he simply accepted the facts of life that only age can reveal. "They suspected it was an aneurysm in the brain. There was nothing anyone could have done for her."

Lyle pulled a napkin from the dispenser and handed it to me. I dabbed my eyes, trying to save my mascara as best I could.

"So, you have no one to cook for you but Mateo. That's the saddest part of this entire story."

"Hey!" Mateo surprised me again with his presence. This time he was leaning against the register, apparently eavesdropping.

"Would you stop lurking? Go cook something."

"For whom?" He motioned to the empty diner.

"For me, I haven't eaten yet."

"What you want?"

"Anything."

Mateo grumbled and went back into the kitchen to cook me something. I looked at Lyle, who was watching me. "I don't eat here because I can't cook," he said. "I eat here because it reminds me of her."

"I wish I could know what that feels like. I've lost a lot of people over the years and I can't think of one place that reminds me of them."

Lyle shook his head. "If you don't stay in one place long enough, you never will."

I smiled and looked out the window. Across the parking lot, the lights of the gas station had turned on, filling the area with an unsightly yellow glow. "You're very astute, Lyle, but I'm afraid my bed has been made and slept in already."

"It worries me to see such a young person with so many burdens."

I laughed. "You can't tell me it gets easier with age."

"No, but it does get easier with faith."

I took a breath and looked back at him. "If by faith you mean a strong belief in God, then I have that. More than I need, actually. However, if you mean faith as in assurance that everything will turn out okay... Then no, I don't have any of that. I doubt I deserve for everything to turn out okay."

"You shouldn't do that."

"What, doubt my worth?"

"No, that." Lyle nodded down to my arm, which I was stabbing with a steak knife.

I gasped and forced my hand to stop. Despite the gauze bandage, my misbehaving right hand had snagged Lyle's knife and was puncturing my skin with the tip of the knife. Though I hadn't felt it before, I realized my pain the moment I saw blood seep through the wrapping.

"Son of—ahhh!" I tossed the knife away and stretched my fingers. I resisted the urge to punch myself in the face since, at the moment, it would still be all my pain. I scooted out of the booth and picked up the coffee canister. I also grabbed the knife back, since it was now contaminated with my blood. I slipped it into my apron pocket and covered my mouth before speaking to Lyle. "I'm so sorry, Lyle. My crazy doesn't always stay locked up. I'll get you a new knife."

"No, no, no." He waved me away. "I'm done, anyway. Just the check."

"Forget the check. I'll pay for your dinner. It's the least I can do."

He thought about that for a moment and narrowed his eyes. "My wife once told me that you can never have too much faith, but even a sliver of doubt is too much. Maybe what you need isn't more faith, but less doubt."

I nodded appreciatively and took his dirty dishes back into the kitchen to be washed.

Chapter 4

Less doubt? Easier said than done, I thought as I headed into the bathroom to check my new wounds. I closed the door to the miniature room that barely fit a sink and toilet. As I removed the bandages, I glimpsed myself in the mirror. I was glaring sadistically. "This is getting ridiculous, Hennie," I scolded my former self. "What do you want?"

I relaxed my body, allowing her to control my movements. She raised my hand slowly and swiped a finger across my throat. I grimaced and shook my head. "Yes, I know you want to die. But in order for you to die, *I* have to die."

My reflection shrugged at me.

"Naturally, you have no sympathy for *my* predicament since I've been holding you captive for the last decade and a half," I mumbled more to myself. "I won't allow myself to die. God gave me permission to be here. I believe he has a purpose for me." My reflection flipped me off. "Look, we can argue about this from now until I'm eighty, or we can try to make peace with each other."

My hand slapped across my face hard enough to make my cheekbone throb. I groaned and blinked at my reflection. "Seriously, can you cut me some slack?" My hand came up again, but I took control of the other hand and grabbed it by the wrist. I stood before the mirror, struggling to arm wrestle myself into submission. "Hennie, stop it! You know I can hurt you if I need to."

My arm stopped resisting and released. It fell limply at my side, surrendering to my control. Tears streamed from my eyes. Not my own.

Before I could let the guilt of unconscious actions weigh down my heart, I slipped myself back into the driver's seat and wiped away the tears. I felt terrible about Hennie's situation. She had been in a coma when I had taken her over. An easy mark for possession—or, in this case, assimilation.

Unlike a traditional demonic host, Hennie was not being tormented by me. I did not unnecessarily harm myself or make her do vile things. However, since I completely controlled her body, it was as if she had been in a coma for nearly sixteen years. I couldn't imagine what it was like for her, perpetually waiting to awaken, trapped in a dream state.

If it weren't for her invitation to the beast, she wouldn't have been able to do the things she was doing now. It had given her the strength to fight. And though I hated to admit it, she was getting stronger. Certainly not strong enough to push me out—not without the help of Rachel and Paula—but she was obviously strong enough to cause me harm. Which, in and of itself, could be detrimental to my survival.

The more control she had over my body, the closer she could get to kill herself and me with her. All it would take would be an ill-timed step in a stairwell, or off a curb.

Bam! Dead! And unlike when I had tried to harm myself, it would stick.

The rules about my connection to my shadow were rather complex. I couldn't kill myself without killing him, and since God wouldn't allow that, suicide was off-limits from here on out. And when Dane or Paula or the beast tried to hurt me, it would, in turn, hurt my shadow. The trinity seemed to be independent of one another in this way, but not me. I remained intrinsically connected to the serpent.

However, I could die from an accident or at the hands of an innocent person. I didn't really understand the mechanism that allowed this caveat, but I assumed it had to do with the restrictions placed on demons and the like. Evildoers only affected the part of me that had risen from hell, while humans and Earth-based dangers could only harm my physical being.

At any rate, it meant Hennie, even with a small amount of control, was dangerous to me. I was reluctant to use magical means to subdue her, but more and more it was looking as if I would need to defend myself pre-emptively.

CHAPTER 5

I STEPPED OUT OF the bathroom after rewrapping my gauze and nearly walked into Star, the night waitress. She was a soft-spoken woman with big bottle-blond hair and big fake breasts to match. As a former stripper, she did tremendously well at earning tips despite working the slowest shift. I was almost positive she was doing bathroom lap dances and blow jobs as a side gig, but who was I to judge? I had offered my *services* to two men already today, and I wasn't even getting paid for it.

"Hey, sweetie, there you are. I'm all clocked in. Anything you need me to work on tonight?"

"Oh, yeah." I grimaced. "I didn't get the silverware finished."

"No problem, I got it. Go on home. Get some rest. Oh, did you hurt yourself?" Star gushed over my bandage.

"Yeah, a little. I'll be good as new by tomorrow."

"Okay, well, have a good night." Star headed over to chat with Mateo, who would be on her shift for another few hours. Though Mateo was sweet on me, I had quickly realized I was chopped liver compared to Star.

I grabbed my things and slipped out the back door. I looked around for signs of life, but the only life was at the gas station where two men were laughing and joking about something. Judging by the hand gestures one of them was using, it was something lewd.

I slipped around the side of the building and did another quick check before running into the maze of parked trucks. A few more had arrived since sunset, so there were more places to hide. Good for me, but also good for bad guys. Assuming Pete was still spit-shining his dick, I should have been safe to inspect his trailer without interruption.

The only problem I had was the darkness. It had never occurred to me that it would be hard to locate demons in the dark. There were no shadows if *everything* was a shadow. If not for the security light on the back of the diner, I wouldn't have been able to see two feet in front of me.

Instead of relying on my eyes, I used my instincts. It was easy to feel when my shadow was near because he was inside of me—or vice versa, whatever. However, demons were different; they made the little hairs on the back of my neck rise.

"You need to be careful, Hennie." I jumped at the voice of my shadow. I could barely see him in the reflection of a chrome bumper.

"Don't worry, I won't get you hurt. He's still at the hotel."

"He won't hurt *me*," he said. "He's an innocent."

"What? That guy is dripping with demons."

"Until he's been judged, he's an innocent and he *can* kill you."

"Since when do you care if I die?"

"It's not your death I'm worried about. It's your power. You need to be careful," my shadow insisted.

I also wanted to ask him when he'd started caring about my power usage—since that would ultimately draw my coven and result in me going back to hell—but I didn't want to stop and have a conversation with a bumper. "Yeah, yeah, shut up so I can find his truck."

"Follow the smell of meat," he suggested.

I sniffed the air, doubtful I could actually smell meat, but somehow I could. As I opened myself to the possibility, I awakened senses I shouldn't have—apparently a perk of my powers I hadn't explored yet. Like an overzealous bloodhound, I ran toward the truck that smelled like it had recently left a meatpacking plant. I rounded the back and let out a yelp when I bumped into a man.

I stared at the brown-eyed man I was supposed to be going on a date with at seven o'clock. "There you are," he rumbled with satisfaction. "I thought we said seven."

I checked my watch as if that was the reason I hadn't met with him, not because I was stalking one of my customers. "Oh, yeah, right, sorry... ah..." I gaped at him, suddenly realizing I had never gotten his name.

His mouth parted in a sly smirk, revealing bright white teeth. "My name is Enon."

"I'm Hennie."

"I know. I asked your boss before I left. What are you doing out here? Did you change your mind?"

I wanted to say yes and get him out of my hair, but with his hat off, I could see the piles of brown curls on his head. Curls I wanted so desperately to twist my fingers into. "No," I blurted out. "I just had a little errand to run."

Enon glanced around. "Out here? In the dark? Surrounded by big-rigs?" He raised his chin and stood up a little taller. I hadn't seen him standing when we first met, so his height surprised me. He was even taller than Dane, making me feel diminutive. "All right, Hennie, what's going on? Is this a drug thing? Because I'm not into that kind of fun. I like my women unsedated."

I groaned and shook my head. "I wish it was. I'm sort of spying on someone." I wasn't sure why I was telling him the truth, but I never had been a big fan of lying. Perhaps part of me hated dishonesty in myself because of how much I hated it in others.

"Spying?" he asked. He glanced around to see who might be watching. "Tell me more."

"You see this trailer?" I tapped the back door of the truck we were standing behind.

Enon somewhat mockingly looked over the door. "What of it?"

I bit my lip. "Have you ever met someone and just known they were up to no good?"

Enon reached over and tugged on the chain of my necklace, drawing my tiny cross pendant out from beneath my uniform. "You mean like right now?" He released the cross and let his hand trail down my chest. It should have been a minor tantalization, but it hit me like the warm sun on a wintry day.

It took every ounce of my logical mind to overturn my desire to ride him like a pogo stick right then and there. I moved a little closer to him. "Look, we are going to get to that very soon, but I need to see what's inside this truck first. If you aren't down for breaking and entering, then I suggest you go wait for me at the diner."

I watched him look me over, debating perhaps if I was worth the risk of being arrested. "It's not breaking and entering if it's unlocked." Enon reached over and pulled open the door to the trailer. I frowned at this convenience with disappointment. He shrugged and motioned for me to go inside. "You want me to stand watch?"

"Yeah, just whistle if anyone is coming."

Enon nodded and offered me his linked hands for a lift-up. He boosted me onto the ledge and I pushed through a plastic curtain into the darkness within. The truck was most definitely used to deliver some kind of meat. I hoped it was animal meat. I was certain the distinction between mammals was rather thin.

I jumped when the refrigeration unit kicked on, adding a new batch of cool air to the space. I felt around for something resembling a light switch—assuming there was one. Since I no longer had the luxury of a cell phone, I didn't even have that as an option to light my way.

I hit something cold and heavy. It moved as I touched it. It was hanging. A slab of beef? A half of a pig? Against my better judgment, I groped the plastic bag containing it. I couldn't tell much, but I was reasonably certain this was not a human carcass hanging from a hook inside of a refrigerated beef truck.

Reasonably sure.

After playing bumper cars with a few more meat popsicles, I bumped into a table. I felt the hard, cold ledge of stainless steel. Did this guy butcher his own meat on the fly? My thoughts returned to murder. Was this a kill room? Did people actually do that?

As I moved along the table, I had a thought. I reached up above it, searching the vacant space for a cord. I flagged my arm for several seconds before I slapped a pull string. I batted at it until I could get a proper grip on it. I gave it a firm tug, and a blinding incandescent glow filled the room. I let out a little yelp when I saw dozens of hanging carcasses around the space.

I immediately switched my reaction to a chuckle when I realized how ridiculous I was being. Even if I didn't have greater expectations of myself as a woman, as an incarnation of the devil, I shouldn't be shrieking like a little girl.

I bent down beside the stainless steel table and examined the tools stored beneath it. Cleavers, filet knives, and, of course, the ones that might as well be called kitchen machetes. It all looked relatively normal, considering the man's line of business. It wasn't until I stood up again that I noticed the abnormality.

The silver against silver didn't stand out. Especially down on the leg of the table.

I leaned forward, touching the silver cuff latched around the table leg like a bracelet. The other side clanked against the leg as I shifted it. I looked at the other three corners.

Handcuffs.

The table was equipped with restraints.

There was only one mammal I knew of requiring such precautions. Especially if they were still alive while they were being butchered.

My eyes surveyed the room, looking for more evidence of this heinous crime. I could feel my hackles rise as I thought about the level of pain that had drawn in so many demons thirsty for torment and torture.

The bagged meat around me had been a sea of red muscle and white sinew when I first looked at it, but now I saw them. The three bags tucked in behind the others. Through foggy plastic, six eyes stared back at me. I knew it was only my imagination, but for a split second, I thought I could hear their screams. Their final screams.

I reached down and picked up a chef's knife from under the table. My thoughts turned to what I might cut off this murderer first.

"Hennie!" my shadow's image was barely a blur in the shiny knife blade, but I looked down to see what he had to say. "Look out!" he screamed, but it was too late. Another blur in the reflection came in fast and hit me over the head. I was out before I hit the floor.

CHAPTER 6

I WOKE TO THE feel of cold metal on my back. I tried to sit up, but the handcuffs I'd discovered earlier locked down my wrists and ankles. A low whistle sounded from somewhere behind me. I tipped my head back to see what the trucker might be plotting for me, but instead, I found my so-called lookout.

"Enon," I whispered.

He looked down at me and a smooth smile lit his face. "Welcome back," he said with seemingly sincere delight.

"Are you working with Pete?" I asked. "Was this your plan all along?" I rapped the cuffs loudly against the table as I tried to free myself. I could have broken them the moment I had woken, but I was still trying to avoid unnecessary bloodshed—though that might have been inevitable. Also, I wasn't ready to run again. It was such a pain to relocate.

Enon moved around the table and looked at me with bemusement. "Why do you think that truck driver has anything to do with this?"

"He—" I started to answer but realized I had no Earthly means of knowing what I knew. "This is his truck."

Enon looked around at the container full of hanging corpses—animals and humans alike. "No, this is *my* truck."

I grimaced at my mistake. Why hadn't I seen any demons around him? "You mean your kill room," I said snidely.

Enon groaned and shook his head. "Well, no, not exactly. I mean, yes, people do tend to die in here. And, yes, I have killed a few, but I assure you they were mercy kills."

"How Dr. Kevorkian of you? Listen, I don't know what you plan to do to me, but you have about ten seconds to come to your senses before I devastate that pretty face of yours."

Instead of cowering like I wanted, or even guffawing like a maniacal hyena, Enon just looked at me with an odd mixture of lust and pride. "I have to say, I was more than a little disappointed by how easy you made this for me. I mean, I always planned to get you in here, but I was so hoping we could have an evening together before I had to..." He trailed off and sighed as he looked over my supine body lying on the table before him. He rested his hand on my knee and slowly slid it up my leg, his fingers tickling my inner thigh. "I don't suppose you would be interested in a little bondage play." He locked eyes with me as his fingers reached the V of my body. He offered a delicate stimulation that made me regret checking this truck instead of going back to my hotel room.

Not that I was still interested in him now that I knew he was a serial killer. Clearly, I wasn't a masochist who was only attracted to men with a propensity to kill.

Shit.

"Stop it!" I kicked my legs, and though it didn't technically do anything to repel him, he withdrew his hand. "So, you're willing to kill me, but not rape me?" I asked.

Enon shrugged as if he hadn't really thought about his inconsistent morality. "What can I say? I'm a romantic. Besides, I don't actually intend to kill you—unless you ask me to."

"Is torture really a fair game? I think if I'm an inch deep in my own blood, I will probably beg to die."

Enon once again looked baffled by my accusation. "What torture? What blood?"

I leaned as best I could to look under his table. "The knives, asshole."

Enon looked down and winced. "No. Eww! Those are for the beef. If I have to kill someone, I suffocate them. It's not the most pleasing activity for me, but it is cleaner."

"If you *have* to kill someone?" I clanked my shackles. "Why am I strapped to this table, then? What's left after rape, murder, and torture?"

Enon's enthusiasm returned. "You have no idea what I am, do you?" He shook his head introspectively. "I thought for certain you were aware. How else could you sense the danger in here?"

"Let's skip the twenty questions and you can just tell me who you are and what you want."

"I want to help you," he said. I scoffed. "I'm serious," he said more sternly. He reached over and unwound the bandage that was covering my claw marks and my fresh stab wounds. After he removed it, he leaned over me to caress the wounds. "I can help you, Hennie. I can get that bastard out of you."

My eyes flickered over his. He was close to me. Close enough to smell the first wood fire of winter coming off him. Earth and ash, with a hint of pine. It wasn't a bad smell, but it was unexpected. "Who?" I asked, vaguely remembering what we were talking about.

Enon leaned in slowly, his gaze moving from my eyes to my lips. I considered headbutting him. That was definitely the only appropriate response to this situation. Yes, when a man straps you to a table and threatens to "help" you die, you absolutely don't make out with him.

While I was still debating the most dignified way to handle my captivity, Enon descended on my lips, locking me into a deep, sumptuous kiss that deserved to have a bed to back it up. I considered the idea that I could use a tryst to buy me time to get away, but again, there was no question of if I could get away to begin with. Just turn up the juice and bust a magical cap in this guy's ass.

He rested his arm behind my head, giving me a pillow of sorts. It was kind of sweet—compared to the head-bashing he had given me earlier.

I gave up fighting my urges. I mean, really, what was the difference between killing the guy, or screwing the guy, and *then* killing him? Obviously, he had no issues with this order of events. Then again, should the man holding me hostage get rewarded with sex?

Maybe this was his true torture—get my sugar cravings to the max and then take away my candy. Asshole!

As I suspected, Enon pulled away just as things were getting good. He was panting, and he let out a groan as he moved away from me. "Okay, okay." He paced the table beside me. "I can't do this. I really want to, but being with you will only mess with my head and make it harder to do what needs to be done." Enon didn't seem to be convincing me, but rather himself. "This isn't the easiest of procedures, so I need to stay focused."

"Procedures? What exactly are you planning to do to me?"

"I told you. I'm going to get that evil bastard out of you."

"What…" I stared at him, eyes widening with my belated apprehension. "You think I'm possessed by a demon?"

"I know you are," Enon said with authority. "A pretty strong one, too."

Pretty strong? Please, I was one-quarter devil and all soul, baby. I wasn't just strong, I was nuclear. Not that I got to prove that to anyone—ever.

"You're not an ax murderer. You're an exorcist."

"Actually, no." Enon smiled proudly. "I'm a demon-hunter."

CHAPTER 7

WHILE ENON PREPARED FOR my exorcism, I took to screaming and yelling for help. It was my last-ditch effort to save myself without using my power—lame as it was.

"No one can hear you," Enon said. "Even if the meat in this room wasn't enough to absorb your racket, the spells I've put around it will."

I stopped shouting and looked back at him. He was searching my purse for some reason. "Ahem," I said mockingly. "Do you need a tampon or something?" I asked, slightly more offended by his pilfering than his intent to extract me from my body. Not that I believed for one second he was strong enough, being a mere mortal and all.

He glanced at me. "Sorry, I forgot my lighter at the hotel. Do you have one?"

"You know, if you can't come to your exorcisms prepared, you may want to rethink your line of work."

Enon smiled and dropped my purse. He moved back and leaned over the table, his amusement still tipping the corners of his lips. "Do you have a lighter or not?"

I rolled my eyes and nodded downward. "Apron left pocket."

He reached down and pulled my real fake pack of cigarettes out of my pocket. It had come fully equipped with a lighter when I'd found it. Enon pulled the red plastic lighter out of the pack. He looked at the cigarettes and then at me. "You don't smoke."

"How can you tell?"

"I can't smell it on you." I perked a brow. Apparently, I wasn't the only one with an acute sense of smell. "I smell smoke on you, but it's more like burning flowers."

"Huh, I was thinking the same about you—fire and pine."

Enon's gaze dropped as he thought about this. "Hmm, I guess that makes sense." He moved out of view. I heard the scrape of my lighter, followed by a poof of ignition and the hiss of a propane-fed flame.

"What are you going to do to me?" I asked. "I mean specifically."

"I am going to perform a ceremony that will allow me to pull the demon from inside of you."

"Do you really think you're strong enough to pull me out?"

Enon chuckled. "Aren't *you* the egotistical one?"

"Lately, yes."

"Trust me, I have extracted more than my fair share of demons. You, my dear, will be easy to remove. Honestly, I usually go after more challenging prey, but as you know, my hunt had other priorities."

"That's good to know," I called back to him, since his voice seemed to move farther away from me. "I would hate to think you only wanted me for my demon side. I mean, a girl's gotta be appreciated for her outsides too."

"Oh, I'm pretty sure the bulk of my attraction to you *is* your demon side. It's a shame too, because once I pop you out, I may not even be interested in that body. I mean, I would pump one out if your host is especially grateful, but there usually isn't time."

"Why is that?"

"Well, if your host survives, and I do believe she will since you are such a young possession, then she will still be at risk of repossession." I frowned at the description of *young*. I had been here for over a decade. That wasn't exactly young.

"What's the matter? Only have the stamina for one exorcism a night?" I joked, though I knew very well those subjugated by demons rarely, if ever, stayed free for long. Sister Aggie had usually given her repeat offenders a few days or even weeks, but that was it.

"It's not so much my stamina as it is my appetite that limits me. It's too bad, really, cause at any given time I've got a dozen or more demons waiting for me to open up a spot for them."

Realization dawned on me in two parts. First, I realized this truck wasn't merely a vacuum of pain, but an unemployment office for demon rejects looking to cash an easy paycheck. Second, my slow brain did a double-take on—"Did you just say *appetite*?"

I craned my neck, trying to see what was burning behind me. I was familiar with the many workings of witchcraft, but I hadn't expected Enon to undress. I wasn't sure a single practitioner would be required to observe the tradition of exposure—especially during an exorcism.

As I had suspected, his lack of beer gut was because of a fine set of lean abdominal muscles. He was fit but not brawny like Dane. However, he did have one commendable appendage that matched Dane's body type.

He caught me ogling him and turned to allow me a better view. "You're starting to wish you had stayed at the diner, too." I couldn't really nod in my upside-down position, but I was certain my hungry eyes agreed with him.

After getting his socks off, Enon gathered up his propane torch and burgundy fabric roll that looked like a travel pouch for jewelry. He brought it over to the table, and with little regard to my movement potential, set it next to me. I observed the hot blue flame with a certain degree of concern. Pain would likely prevent me from controlling my reactions. I was either going to have to put a stop to this now or risk doing something I would regret. And yet I was still curious about this man. This demon-hunter.

"What did you mean about appetite?"

Enon frowned at me. "Surely you know what a demon-hunter is. Hasn't your kin warned you about my ilk?"

"I was kind of sequestered in hell. My... kin locked me up pretty tight."

"Mmm." Enon nodded as if he understood my servile predicament. He unrolled his fabric, revealing a collection of metal tools that looked part surgical and part decorative. He pulled one such device from its nook and flipped the flat circle out so it was perpendicular to the handle.

I looked over the embellished disk that now looked like a cookie stamp. Enon placed the metal into the propane flame.

Correction, there will be no cookies. I'm getting branded.

I watched the metal turn orange with heat as Enon spoke. "Have you heard of the fallen?" he asked.

"You mean like fallen angels?" I asked, unable to take my eyes off the brander.

"Yes."

"I've heard of one," I said, enjoying my insider information about my origin.

"Then you must know it goes both ways." I finally looked at him, and Enon's humorless eyes latched onto mine. I saw something there I hadn't expected to see at this moment.

Pain.

"Just as a disgraced angel can fall from the heavens, a repentant demon can rise from hell."

My mouth gaped at this new information. Since this definition also applied to me, I should have known there might be others like me—residents of hell who no longer wanted to be surrounded by the agony that was provided in large eternal doses. "Are *you* risen?" I asked, somewhat hopeful the answer would be yes. I wasn't sure why that made everything he was doing better, but I really wanted Enon to be on the right shoulder instead of the left. Or at least in the neck region.

"I was the first to rise," Enon said almost nostalgically, "and I will be the last to fall." His jaw clenched with determination as he pressed the hot stamp onto the tender flesh at the center of his chest, just above his sternum. He hissed in a breath as his skin sizzled, turning white and then black. After his growling exhale, he lowered the stamp and placed it on the table next to my leg, being careful not to let it touch me.

Enon reached into his collection and pulled out a scalpel. My breathing hastened as he brought it closer to me. I reached for my power but didn't engage. Not yet, I thought. I still didn't have my answers.

His finger dipped beneath my collar and he tugged the fabric away from my neck. He delicately cut the cotton, breaking the hemline. Once he was about an inch down, he put his scalpel back with his tools. His hands returned and grabbed both sides of the rent fabric. He looked at me with determination, but also as if he were waiting for me to give him permission to proceed. I said nothing, but once again, my eyes may have been betraying my inappropriate lust.

His biceps tensed and he yanked the fabric. I gasped, surprised by his ferocity and the sudden exposure to the cool air. I panted under his admiring gaze. Though my bra was a full coverage variety, the cool storage container was allowing him a sneak peek from beneath the thin fabric.

This should not be hot!

I should not have been turned on by a man preparing me for an exorcism.

Seriously, what was wrong with me? I mean, yes, the devil, but come on. When did my survival instincts kick in?

"Isn't it a little hypocritical for you to exorcise demons while you continue to possess your own vessel?" I asked, changing the subject.

Enon seemed to lose interest in my breasts and went back to heating his iron. "I am not a possession." He sounded a little perturbed by my accusation.

"But you've risen from hell."

"The risen are not possessors. We do not share bodies with humans."

"But you're human." Enon glanced at me, giving me a rather severe look as if I was insulting him. I frowned at any suggestion that he wasn't human. "How did you take corporeal form if not by possession?"

"A very complex form of conjuring that is not only difficult to achieve but almost impossible to maintain," he explained, though it told me very little. He pulled the iron from the flame and looked at me. "Are you ready?"

I looked at the blazing hot stamp. Of course, I wasn't ready to be burned. What did I look like, a cow about to go to slaughter? It was time to use my power, but even as I considered my escape, I noticed the circular pucker on Enon's chest. The swirling design meant nothing to me, but I understood the mechanism behind it. Much like a blood ceremony that speeds up the process of the magic, this branding ceremony would effectively bond us. I had no doubt he would use this to his advantage while extracting my soul, but something about the idea of merging with him appealed to me on a deeper level.

Innuendos to sex aside, I missed my magical connection to my sisters more than I wanted to admit to myself. It had been easier when I'd had Dane to use for stress relief, but out here on the road, I only had Hennie and my shadow to satisfy my need for interdependency and friendship. And frankly, they were both shit at it.

I took in a deep breath and this time I did nod my permission for him to continue. I wondered if he could have proceeded without my permission, but it didn't matter now. The moment I agreed, I became the facilitator of this magic as much as its victim.

He didn't seem surprised by my compliance, but rather titillated by it. He reached his unarmed hand forward and pushed it behind my neck. He pulled me upward, which drew my chest up even while my head leaned back, exposing my neck and broadening his target. He moved the iron over my sternum and I locked eyes with him. He seemed to be feeling as many conflicting emotions as me. As if this hunger was more than just the physical craving we obviously had for one another.

He pressed the stamp against my skin and for a split second, it felt cold as ice. I could hear the sizzle of my skin and I could smell chicken feathers, but there was no pain. My eyes flickered over the man above me—the very talented occultist who was masking my pain. Judging by his clenched jaw and pursed lips, he was transferring it to himself.

He removed the hot brand and took a few calming breaths. I felt the throb of the after-burn, but it was minimal because the deep scorching of my skin had numbed the nerves. "Thank you," I said, knowing full well he did not have to take that extra step to complete the bond.

"I have no desire to hurt you, Hennie. I'm here to help you."

"Like you helped them." I nodded back to the three dead faces hanging among the slabs of beef.

Enon looked back at the corpses and frowned. He shook his head. "The first two were weak. They didn't survive the extraction process. They were old possessions. The human body was not meant to endure such stresses." He tipped his chin toward the body in the far corner. "The last one was a mercy kill."

"You killed her?"

"She asked me to. She begged me," he said rather insistently, denying any guilt in his action, even though he was looking at the corpse like he was remembering the woman's last moments of life. "The possessed live pathetic lives, trapped inside of others. Never being able to emerge. Never having control. It's endless torture. *Debra* was one of those victims." Enon spoke her name as if he were reciting a list of fallen war heroes—giving voice to her name out of honor instead of pity.

I wondered if he would do the same for Hennie. Would he revere her struggle? Would he view her passing as a noble, sacrificial end?

"You're wrong about this body surviving," I said. "Hennie is weak."

Enon chuckled and shook his head. "Hennie is very strong. Her soul is the strongest I've ever felt. Your essence is the weak one, so withered and distorted that it looks splintered."

Splintered? Did my separation from the trinity splinter my soul? Did that make it weak? Last I checked, I was stronger than ever. Could it be? Had I gotten a bum soul?

Enon leaned forward and whispered, "All I see inside you is anger."

Anger?

My eyes flickered over his, widening with a new level of concern.

Enon may have been a demon-hunter, but he obviously wasn't very good at it. The human soul he thought he was sensing was my own fallen, fractured, and risen one. Powerful and permissible, but by no means the rightful owner of this vessel.

The weak splinter presence he was sensing was actually Hennie. The beast she'd invited in to assist her death must have been masking her humanity and making her appear to Enon as an evil presence. His assumption was that Hennie was *my* demon possessor.

As much as I wanted to correct his misconception, I wondered if an exorcism could work for me—for us. Could Enon actually remove a human soul from its rightful place on Earth? And if so, would I be rejected on principle? Surely, I wasn't bound to Hennie's soul, only her body. If she left, I would be the only viable soul, therefore... Party of one!

I could free myself from Hennie's suicidal attempts at murder and she could be free, just like she wanted. It was a win-win. Unfortunately, it was a risk. I couldn't exactly ask Enon about the mechanics of his extraction. If he knew I was the possessor, he might well adjust his aim and go after me instead.

There was only one way to do this right. We had to make this decision together, Hennie and I.

I wasn't sure how Hennie's presence worked. Could she see everything I saw? Could she hear it all? Could she even hear my thoughts or sense my emotions? Regardless, I needed to talk to her.

I released my grip on my body and relaxed into the back seat—so far as my limbs, anyway. I still needed my mind in the driver's seat.

"I wonder how Hennie feels about this?" I asked Enon, though I was actually speaking to her. "This exorcism could give her what she's always wanted. Her freedom. To be away from me once and for all."

"In my experience, hosts are always relieved to have the burden of possession lifted from them."

"Exactly. I wonder if she would be willing to take on the risk of the extraction for the possibility of being herself again." Enon gave me a sidelong glance as he circled the table, placing amulets around my body.

I waited, hoping she would give me a sign. Something I could even vaguely interpret as approval. My fist jumped up, clanking the cuffs against the table. I looked at the fingernails digging in hard against the palm—perpetually pissed off since her merge with the beast. Anger that she had suppressed for far too long.

The thumb slowly rose, pointing at the ceiling. I took a steadying breath; thankful she was on board. I nodded and relaxed back on the table. "Okay, I'm ready," I said, mostly to myself. "I'm ready to be set free."

"Oh, I'm afraid you won't be going free." Enon stopped at my head and placed his hands on my forehead as if he were about to perform a theatrical psychic reading.

"What? What do you mean? You're extracting the demon, aren't you?"

Enon scoffed, followed quickly by a chuckle. He looked down at me, brow dipped as if he couldn't understand how a demon had come to be so stupid. "I'm not a priest. I'm a hunter. I told you, maintaining this form takes a great deal of effort. I need the energy to support myself. Once I extract you from this body, I will use you as sustenance."

"Sustenance!" I squawked. "You're gonna eat me!"

CHAPTER 8

I WAS BACK TO screaming, but it did me little good. Enon latched onto me through our branded link. I could feel his strength and intensity. While my connection to the coven had exuded a groovy power-of-the-universe feel, Enon injected a raw Mother Earth vibe into me. It certainly wasn't as strong, but it was authoritative. Despite the danger he posed, I couldn't help but enjoy his powerful presence being inside of me.

Even as I felt his grip on me tighten, I felt my grip on Hennie weaken. Her little soul was getting slippery, and having never been on this side of an exorcism, I wasn't sure how to keep hold of her.

As much as I wanted to have this body to myself, I did not want Hennie to be eaten. She needed to be set free. I would not let her endure any more torture at my hands or anyone else's. I focused on my power and latched onto her, but I felt something awful when I did, as if daggers were digging into my back.

I let out another cry and Enon shushed me. "It's going to be okay, Hennie. The demon is fighting, but I will get it out. I promise."

His words should have reassured me, but they mortified me. This was all backward. He was going to extract a human soul and eat it. I was no one to judge a person's dietary preferences, but if anyone was going to get eaten, it should have been the wicked little bastards flying over this truck, not Hennie's innocent little soul.

I pulled back harder, and I felt something give, but not in a good way.

"No, no, no," Enon babbled. "Don't break. Just come on out."

Break? Could Hennie break? What happens if she breaks?

I had to think. Hennie was obviously a weak soul. This tug of war would kill her before Enon could. She needed strength. She needed to be healed.

For the first time since I came into this body, I let go. I released the grip I had unconsciously held for well over a decade. As I did, I sensed her. I felt her soul expand as if she were being reborn.

It was a tactical risk, but I pressed my power into her, giving her enough strength to hold her position in this body if she wanted to. I felt eyes on me and my vision doubled. Though I should have only seen the ceiling of the truck, I could now see myself. I was lying on this table staring up at the eyes that were staring down at me—an out-of-body experience combined with an in-body experience.

"Oh, you've got some hidden strength, do you?" Enon observed. "Good, so do I."

With delicacy no longer an issue, Enon grabbed onto Hennie's soul and yanked on it with a good deal more force than he had been using.

All at once, Hennie slipped from my grasp. The double vision ceased, and the knives in my back dragged downward until they reached the base of my spine and stuck there, intensifying in pain with every second.

Having had enough of the damsel routine, I grabbed my power and broke the handcuffs holding me in place. I flipped over and reached out for Hennie's soul. I snagged the equivalent of her pinky toe and held on for dear life, trying not to hurt her even as I kept her away from the jaws of death.

Time slowed, and I felt my movements become heavy as if I were pushing against setting concrete. There was no longer any distinction between the real world and the magical one. There were demon shadows all around us, looming in the eaves, waiting for a position to open up.

Enon looked different. He was an overlapping image of human and amorphous blob. What I assumed to be his mouth was opening wide, ready to consume Hennie's soul.

While he appeared as a double image, I was tripled—or quadrupled, if you counted my current position. I could see myself down on the table receiving a scalp massage, but I was also in the process of breaking free. Following my current position, I was also being drawn into the mouth of the demon hunter. My final blurred image—the one being eaten, looked back at me.

This was Hennie.

This was the girl, now a woman, who had taken the back seat to her life because of me.

It amazed me to see her looking at me with anything less than virile anger. If anything, she was looking at me with pity. She was about to be eaten alive and *she* pitied *me*?

I felt the pain in my back release, only to radiate up higher. I looked back to see the cause of my new agony.

Then I saw the reason for Hennie's pity. It wasn't daggers in my back; it was claws. The beast—manifested as a lion—was clawing its way up my back like a house cat climbing a tree. It was no doubt unhappy with losing its vessel. I winced as it retracted its claws, only to drive them back in again.

I ignored the pain as best I could and turned my attention back to Hennie. My grip on her was tenuous at best. If I pulled her back in, she would be a prisoner again. If I let her go, she would be demon food. I didn't know what to do. I didn't know what the right decision was. Though time had slowed significantly, Hennie was still moving toward her death. I sensed I had to decide quickly or fate would decide for me.

I hated myself for waiting so long to take action. What good was power if you couldn't use it to help people?

I considered killing Enon, but he wasn't a human. Whatever a risen was, they weren't weak. Besides that, our temporary connection made it almost impossible for me to want to harm him, let alone *actually* harm him.

Hennie seemed to reach the same conclusion. Her face turned somber as she looked back at the void she was facing, care of a growing cavern of darkness inside of Enon. She looked at me and nodded.

Nodded?

Was she actually giving me permission to let her die? Not sent to heaven on angels' wings, but just forever and ever not to exist?

This realization robbed me of the very breath in my lungs. The stabbing pain in my back was nothing to that of the ache in my heart. Hennie was choosing perpetual nothingness over the prison I had created for her.

At that moment, I couldn't understand anything. I didn't understand why I had avoided bearing witness to the atrocities of hell, only to rise to Earth and torture another. And why had God allowed me to stay? Why, when he had to know the pain Hennie was in, did he let me continue to inhabit her? But most of all, I wondered why I thought God's permission should alleviate any guilt I had at doing so.

At the bottom of my veritable barrel, I found the answer I had been avoiding since I'd discovered my origins. I had to go back to the devil. I had to release Hennie. I had to let go of this body.

With me tethered to Enon, the beast still clawing at Hennie, and me holding onto her so she didn't fall into the abyss, I couldn't simply let go of her or pull her. I needed to focus my power on cutting my connection to this body so Hennie could fall back into it and be safe. I also needed to make sure when I left, I took the beast with me, so she could be free of its influence—not to mention scare off the demon rabble that was frothing at the thought of getting into her after I left. All without obliterating the entirety of four city blocks in the process.

As I considered how to make that happen, I remembered the knife in my apron pocket. I pulled it out and looked at the blood on the blade. My blood. Hennie's blood.

With the help of a little old-school magic, I wrapped the energy I needed to cut my cord around the blade. I bound the energy to the blood, which in this case represented an expedited consent. It would quicken the process of severing myself from this world. I also added a little cleansing aftershock that would roast some demon pricks upon my exit. Too bad I wouldn't be around for that part of the show.

I reached out to the beast, encouraging it to grab on tight with my magical equivalent of a taunt. Since it wasn't much of a thinker, it didn't know it was playing right into my plan.

I was pretty darn proud of my strategy. I looked back at Hennie—who was on the verge of entering the darkness within Enon. She looked shocked and baffled. I wasn't sure if she understood the sacrifice I was about to make, but she understood what it meant. I was about to die for her. I put on a simpering smile—pleased as punch to once and for all be the hero of the story.

I raised the steak knife and swiped it down between myself and the body that was still lying on the table beneath me. My physical—Hennie's physical form.

I felt the connection between myself and Hennie snap. Unfortunately, I'd underestimated Enon's grip on me. Even as he was trying to rip Hennie out, he was grounding me to this body—preventing me from being dragged out during the exorcism. In the end, I had done the exact opposite of what I wanted. Hennie was going to get eaten, anyway. And now that I had disconnected myself, I had no way of saving her. What little grip I had on her released.

Normal time and movement returned, and I heard Enon say, "What the fuck?"

Then something exploded.

CHAPTER 9

I WOKE AGAINST THE wall of the trailer, alive though not necessarily well. My head was throbbing, my heart was racing, and I was thoroughly confused. As I tried to piece together what had happened, I realized one definite fact.

Hennie was gone.

Her soul, as quiet as it had been for so many years, was missing, and her absence was deafening. I should have been thrilled to have this body to myself, but a different emotion overwhelmed me.

I felt empty.

For the first time—possibly in all of my existence pre/post-separation—I was alone. The vacuous sensation of a single mind was terrifying, so much so that I doubled over and let out a stuttered croaking groan just to hear my voice.

Was this what it was like to be human? Was this what it was like to be birthed into life on this Earth? No wonder children can cry long before they can speak. Their tears are evidence of grief, a sorrow endured for ninety years because of a mind locked away from all others.

"What was that?" Enon shifted off the floor where he had landed. "Christ, it smells like barbecue in here."

I looked around, now noticing the smell of cooked meat. I didn't know what happened, but the event had released enough energy to burn the beef hanging in the truck. It occurred to me that it may have been my fault since I'd infused my spell with an aftershock to destroy the demons, but I certainly hadn't put *that* much energy into it.

Enon looked slightly charred, much like me, but I doubted his burns would last long since he had enough magic to heal himself. When he saw me, his brow dipped in confusion. "Why didn't that work?" he asked.

"Because of you, you son of a bitch!" I lunged at him, prepared to rip Hennie clean out of his throat if I had to. Despite my attempts, however, I fell at his feet, exhausted by the mere effort of keeping myself upright.

"What?" he asked, looking down at me.

"You killed her!"

"Her?" My anger baffled him.

"You ate her!" At long last, I found my voice and my power and used them as one. I rose from the floor and brandished my fiery red aura for Enon to see. He blinked at me and the rage on my face, but he didn't cower away.

"What are you?" he asked.

"I am the bastard demon that has been possessing this body."

"No." He denied my words outright. "You aren't a demon. Are you—"

"Going to kill you for eating Hennie's soul? Yes."

I raised my hands to exert my power, but my appendages went just about anywhere but where I wanted to aim them.

"That was a soul?" Enon groaned and rubbed his face. "No wonder this place looks like the inside of an oven." Unintimidated by my defenses, he walked away to gather his things, including his jeans, which he slipped on but didn't zip.

"Why can't I move?" I asked, still trying to go after him.

Enon circled the table, collecting his magical amulets. "We're still connected. You can't hurt me until that burn heals."

"We'll see about that." I pressed my hand to my burn mark and forced my power into it, urging it to heal. Enon stopped what he was doing and leaned on the table. When I moved my hand, I saw that not only had I not healed the wound, but I had made it pucker even more.

"What is this, day one of magic for you?" Enon asked. "You can't undo on the body what is contracted by the mind." He moved closer to me and dipped his head, putting us nose to nose. "Don't worry, it will heal in time and then you will be perfectly capable of *trying* to kill me. Assuming you still want to."

"I'm not likely to forgive you for eating an innocent soul."

Enon took a long breath. All the while, his eyelids twitched in frustration. "I did not eat that soul."

Some of my anger stood aside to make room for curiosity. "You didn't?"

"No, don't be ridiculous. I can't do that."

"You can't? But you eat demons."

"No, I—it's not like eating actual food. It's like fuel. The difference between diesel and unleaded." He motioned toward the front of the semi-trailer. "I can only run on diesel."

"What happened to her then? Why did she... explode?"

Enon laughed and looked me over. "You really *have* been sheltered, haven't you?"

"Yes," I freely admitted.

Enon's more subtle amusement returned to his eyes. "Allow me to teach you then." He put his things back down on the table and picked through them to get his shirt out. Instead of putting it on himself, he started dressing me in it. I had long since forgotten he had ripped the top of my waitress uniform open. "You see, there is only one kind of battery that can run the human body. And that battery is the soul." Enon started buttoning his shirt on me from the bottom up. "And as you might imagine, there is quite of bit of power in a soul. Even more so when it isn't being burdened by the inane tasks of the human body."

His hands reached the last few buttons, and he slowed his movements. He watched me hungrily as he intentionally let his hands slide along my breasts while he fiddled with the last few. "That soul may have been weak, but it is still stronger than the confines of earthly physics. What you just witnessed and felt was a soul transcending to heaven. Bam!" Enon snapped his fingers, making me jump. "She's all gone. Safe and sound. However, that begs a very big question I'm afraid needs an answer. If the soul is gone and you're still here, that means you're not a demon. So, I'll ask you again. What are you?" Enon leveled a scolding glare at me like I was in trouble for misbehaving.

"I'm something broken," I answered.

"You don't look broken."

"I feel very broken."

Enon's disapproval turned to sympathy. "I know you do." He touched the burn mark on his chest. "I can feel that from you."

"You can?" I touched my emblem, wondering why I couldn't sense his emotions.

"Can you feel me?" I shook my head. "Find yourself." He pulled my hand to his chest and placed his on mine. "Your emotions are too high. Empty your thoughts and look for me. I know you feel angry, alone, and betrayed. Given that this body has undergone a monumental shift in power, you have every right to feel that way, but right now, you aren't alone. I'm right here with you. Beside you and inside of you."

I let go of my mind and focused on his heart beating under my hand. I could feel my pulse aligning with his. Beat for beat, they synced until I couldn't tell the difference between my heart and his. Next, our breathing became one. And then I felt him.

No wonder my first awareness after losing Hennie had been my solitude. There was little difference between my recent loss and Enon's years and years on Earth without friends, family, or even a partner. He would claim to be a loner, but deep inside of him, he was lonely. Just like me. Escaped from hell. Just like me. In need of connection. Just like me.

I looked up at Enon. The hunger inside of me had returned and I could see it reflected in his gaze. Our attraction had only intensified with the bond.

The shirt he had just put on me ejected buttons everywhere. Enon wasted no time with the uniform beneath. His forceful grip completed the rent in the fabric, down to the skirt hem. He lifted me onto the table and jumped up after me. He gave my bra and pants the same treatment, making them useless, but I didn't care.

He buried his face in my chest, suckling hard at the tender flesh. He reached between my legs, penetrating me and stimulating me at the same time. I moaned and arched, trying to get more even though I already had more than I could handle.

His hand retracted and he placed himself between my legs. He pressed into me, giving me even more reason to groan. Enon rocked against me in a quick rhythm until he exhausted my first euphoric cries. Seemingly dissatisfied with our current mode of take-me-now, he pulled me up into his lap. I wrapped my arms around his neck to maintain my straddled position.

"Look at me," he insisted, putting a pause on our pleasures. He looked at me with a sort of concern I didn't understand. "Find me." He placed his hand over my chest. Though I wasn't sure I relished the idea of experiencing our mutually shared loneliness, I did as he asked. I placed my hand on his mark and searched for him in my mind. "There you are," he said and urged me back into movement.

As much enjoyment as I got from round one, the second and third rounds came together almost simultaneously through our connection. They spilled into round four and somewhere between five and six, I found myself in the bed of my hotel room.

I wasn't entirely sure if he had somehow transported us there, or if I had, but one thing was certain: a magical leap that strong was bound to attract the wrong kind of attention.

Not that I cared at that moment. Enon was insatiable, and our connection made our barbaric sexual encounter seem like transcendent lovemaking.

When I eventually reached the dizzy, dehydrated stage, I unmounted and fell face-first into my pillow. Enon curled up beside me and pulled the blankets over us. He leaned into my ear and whispered something I didn't understand. It sounded a bit like a spell, but I didn't care. All I wanted was sleep.

CHAPTER 10

AT SOME POINT IN the night, I woke to someone poking my nose. "Dane," I grumbled and pushed his hand away. I quickly remembered that Dane had not been a resident in my bed for nearly six months. "Enon?" I questioned, even as my eyes flapped open to look at Jess sitting on the edge of the opposite twin bed.

I smiled at my friend, though she didn't look as happy to see me. It had been a while since I'd had a visit from my favorite ghost—and formerly living best friend. She sighed at me and motioned to Enon. "What happened to Dane?"

I glanced back at Enon, who was curled around me. After some effort to extract myself, I sat up on the edge of my bed. "Dane is hunting me down to kill me. I thought it was a good enough reason to break up with him."

"Yeah, but he was hot."

"Enon's hot."

"I guess," she grumbled, as if she was only agreeing not to insult my choice of bed partner. I knew Jess preferred larger men, but I was surprised she was pushing her preferences on me. Until tonight, I hadn't been sure I had any preference. Apparently, I liked bad boys—really bad boys. Or maybe I liked damaged boys.

"This isn't the first time I've hooked up with someone since Dane. Where were you then to lecture me?"

Jess stood up and walked around the hotel room. "I came to warn you that you're in danger."

"Yeah, I know. Too much magical energy has been thrown around. I'll have to get on the road as soon as possible." I glanced at the clock. Three o'clock seemed a little early for an escape. Maybe I could wait a couple of hours and get my continental breakfast before I left.

"That's not what I came to warn you about," Jess said solemnly.

I frowned at the severity of her expression. She looked downright mournful. "What is it?" I stood up and walked to her. I reached out, unsure if I should, or even could, touch her, though she didn't seem to have any trouble touching me. The moment I touched her hands, I immediately felt at ease, even though she was about to give me bad news. "What's wrong?"

"What you did for Hennie's soul was admirable. The sacrifice you were willing to make... Well, I'm proud of you."

"Am I in trouble for staying in this body? Is He mad?" I asked, mortified that I had done anything to piss off the Big Guy.

Jess put on a lopsided smirk and shook her head. "No. He thinks this is a rather fortuitous event—with the exception of one particular loose end. One very dangerous loose end." Jess's eyes trailed away from mine, looking at something behind me.

I turned to look at Enon on the bed. I shrugged. "If he's risen, doesn't that make him kind of good? He can't be any worse than a spiritually reformed serial killer," I rationalized, though it didn't make my choice of men seem any better.

When I looked back, Jess was gone. It was only me, staring at my reflection in the mirror behind the television. My shadow was now perched on the vacant bed, staring at me with the same concerned look as Jess had. He shook his head slightly and deepened his frown. "Oh, Hennie. What have you done?" he asked with abject disappointment in his voice.

My shadow turned to look in the same direction Jess had, but I got the sense that Enon was not the issue. I shifted my position in front of the mirror, searching the pseudo-world inside the frame for the answer to that very question.

It took a moment for me to see. The shift in the shadow within a shadow. The inhuman eyes piercing the veil of blackness. The rhythmic and insistent tail swatting against the wood-paneled walls—matching the increasing beat of my heart. A low growl vibrated my eardrums even as the smell of ash reached my nose.

I slowly turned back to check the corner of the room, but it was empty. The beast was not here in this room with me. It was inside of me. Just as my shadow was ever a part of me, so now was the beast.

I suddenly understood the concern in Jess's eyes. During my attempt to free Hennie's soul, I had grabbed onto the beast—effectively preserving the possession that was meant for Hennie's soul. Since we were one and the same, it wasn't a true possession, but that didn't mean its presence would be harmless.

The beast was the essence of the devil's anger—a rage so great it had fostered the creation of hell and split the devil into thirds. And now that anger was inside of me.

I was already the most powerful being on Earth. Now I was the most volatile one too.

CHAPTER 11

I AWOKE FROM MY dream turned nightmare knowing that it had been neither. I may have gotten rid of one tormenting soul, but I had replaced it with the ferocity of a lion. Setting aside the fact that I had never been the nicest person to begin with, I would certainly turn into a bitch now.

Even as the sweat of my heated dream trickled down my forehead, a cold shiver ran through my body. I opened my eyes and turned to look at the sliver of orange light peeking through the hotel curtains. It was already morning. I hadn't even remembered lying back down.

"Shit!" I hissed and flung off my blankets. Enon's arm, unfortunately, didn't move so easily. "Good God, you weigh a ton," I grunted as I pushed him off.

"What's wrong?" he mumbled as I fell out of the bed onto the floor.

"The magic. It's like a beacon to them. They'll be able to find me now." I raced to the bathroom—despite my haste, I still needed to empty my bladder.

"Who?"

"My coven—my former coven. And..." I trailed off, not ready to get into the complexities of Paula or Paul—aka the walking, talking devil on Earth. Why did my life have to be so odd? Why couldn't I have normal friends who weren't the devil or minions of God? I suddenly relished the idea of bake sales and PTA meetings even though I didn't have kids. It just sounded so blissfully mundane.

"You have a coven?" he asked as he yawned.

"I did." I finished up my morning ablutions and started stuffing my toiletries into my attaché case.

"Is that what you are?" Enon pushed open the bathroom door and leaned on the jamb. "Are you a witch?"

I thought about that and waggled my head. "I guess that's what I am." That was an easier description than the truth and would have to do for now. "Mostly I'm just a fugitive."

"Ooh," Enon droned as if the pieces of this puzzle were falling into place. "Who did you kill?"

I glared at him before brushing past him. "I didn't kill anyone." I looked around but found very little of last night's clothing on the floor. "What happened last night?" I asked, gathering up what little grease-free clothing I had.

"What do you mean?" Enon moved around the room, picking up his own clothes and getting dressed. His shirt was missing, so he helped himself to one of mine. He didn't seem to have any objection to the taut fabric across his chest. I couldn't help but think that Dane would rip clean through my shirts before he could get one on. Not that I was comparing.

"I mean, one second we're banging on a table—the next we're here in my bed."

"Yeah, that was unexpected," Enon said flatly.

"Are you saying that wasn't your doing?"

"Teleportation? Are you serious?"

"You can perform exorcisms, but not teleport?"

"Wow." Enon looked at me with awe. "You really are a beginner, aren't you? How are you even a witch?"

"I told you. I had a coven. We did everything together. I only know what they taught me." I shoved my clothes into my duffle bag. My entire life now fit into a piece of carry-on luggage. How depressing.

"They didn't get very far, did they?"

"No, there were some unforeseen circumstances and then they kicked me out... stripped me of the connection." I grabbed my toiletry bag from the bathroom and tossed it in with the rest of my things.

"Ouch, that's a pretty big kick in the face." Enon perked his brow. "So, who did you kill?"

"Ugh! I didn't kill anyone!" That was a lie, of course. I had killed a handful of people while under the direction of the devil. People I'd thought deserved to die. People I'd thought I had the right to punish, because I'd had the power to do so. I didn't really feel bad that they were dead, but I also had no desire to pursue further work as the devil's judge, jury, and executioner.

"You don't get kicked out of a coven for curling your hair wrong. You either slept with somebody you shouldn't have, killed somebody you shouldn't have, or..."

"Or what?" I tucked in a few straggling sleeves and zipped up my bag.

"Or you have to betray them in some way."

I paused, considering that description. "I didn't betray them, but I did disappoint them." I locked eyes with Enon, who didn't seem sympathetic to my situation, but I got the sense he understood the loss I was feeling. "They disappointed me too," I added with more than a pinch of bitterness in my voice.

Enon's mouth tipped slightly. "Let's go get breakfast." He moved to usher me away from my bag.

"I can't. I need to get out of here right now." I slung my bag over my shoulder.

"You have a vehicle?" he asked.

"No, but I can either steal one or catch a ride with a trucker." I suddenly realized I needed to get dressed. I was still in my nightshirt. I put my bag down and pulled out a pair of jeans along with a button-up shirt.

"You can catch a ride with me then."

"With you?" I asked, dumbfounded. "Why?"

Enon scoffed. "You mean last night isn't reason enough?"

"Last night was great, but I'm on the run." I rushed to put my clothes on and ended up buttoning the shirt incorrectly.

"And I'm a truck driver who doesn't actually work for a trucking company. I can take you to where you need to go. On the road and off it." He nodded to the bed.

I had to admit, his proposition intrigued me. My life had become rather lonely lately. However, I knew involving anyone in my predicament was a bad idea. "Look, Enon. I think it's better for you if you stay away from me. I'm bad news."

"Oh, I know. Why do you think I'm so drawn to you?"

I grimaced at him. "Yeah, that's not really a turn-on for me. Creepy stalker boyfriends are kind of a hard no for me." I grabbed my bag and made it to the door before I realized my purse was still in Enon's truck. I would have to grab it before I took off. Unfortunately, it meant I might run into someone I knew. That usually meant questions about my obvious exit. I hated questions. I never had the answers to satisfy them.

With three or four things running through my mind, I opened the door to the motel room and nearly ran into the man on the other side. I looked up at the tall, broad, muscled chest before me. His blond hair had grown out some, making it messier than I remembered it. His eyes were still the same dreamy blue, though.

"Dane."

CHAPTER 12

I STOOD THERE, BLANK-FACED and dumbfounded by his presence. Even though I'd expected to be found at some point, it was still a shock to see him. I looked over his black waistcoat and V-neck t-shirt. By the looks of the ink peeking through his collar, he had gotten a tattoo since I'd last seen him. Everything about him seemed to be contrary to his boy-next-door image. He finally looked like the dark hunter the coven had cast him to be. He looked like the bad guy—except he wasn't.

I was.

"Who's this?" Enon noticed my stall at the door and came to interject himself into the silent standoff.

Dane's eyes caught on him, taking him in like a brick to the face. Enon just being in my motel room was enough to warrant the hardened expression on his face, but my disheveled appearance only added to the fucked-some-other-guy imagery. When his eyes finally landed on me, he lost all appearance of compassion. "It's time to go, Hennie."

I shook my head, but Enon spoke before I could. "She's not goin' anywhere, friend."

Dane shifted his attention back to Enon as he pushed in close behind me, all but flopping an arm over my shoulder in a show of boyfriend territory. It rather surprised me, since I was still running under the assumption that last night had been a one-night stand, but perhaps I underestimated Enon's capacity for relationships. "This has nothing to do with you... friend," Dane said coolly.

"As of last night, anything to do with Hennie has to do with me." Enon yanked down his collar, revealing the brand on his chest. I had forgotten about it and wondered if that was why he was being so protective. Perhaps the bond demanded it.

Dane's face blanked as he looked at the scorched skin. He turned his attention back to me, or rather my chest. He raised his hand slowly and shifted the fabric aside, revealing some of my cow-brand. I wasn't sure anything could be more jarring to him than finding me with another man, but this seemed to be the cherry on top. I might as well have flashed a ruby engagement ring and told him I was pregnant.

Dane's jaw clenched tightly and his eyes shifted to the floor for a moment before he regained his composure enough to speak. "I see you've been enjoying your time away."

I rolled my jaw and glanced at Enon. I wanted to ask him to back off, but I got the sense he wouldn't or couldn't. He pinned his gaze on Dane, studying his features as if planning to memorize them for a police lineup later.

"I kind of figured our last conversation constituted a breakup. You know—the one where you could no longer control your killer instincts."

To my surprise, Dane smiled at me. "If you think that little charm over your door was the only thing keeping me from killing you that day, then you have seriously underestimated my love for you."

Bam!

There it was. A big fat emotional turd being dropped on my doorstep. It might as well be in a flaming bag, too. Since I couldn't step on it without making a colossal mess, I changed the subject.

"Where's Rachel? I thought she would be here to drag me out by my hair."

Dane looked annoyed that I hadn't responded to his affirmation of love. There would be no hearts melting today. Not while my very existence was in question. I knew people spoke of love being complicated, but I thought my situation had trumped Romeo and Juliet. Screw feuding families and dickhead dads, my love story was going against the natural order. I was the mule among mares. I was the curly fry at the bottom of the fry pile. I shouldn't be here. And yet...

"She sent me ahead. I thought if I had a moment to speak to you, I could convince you to come with us peacefully."

I barked out a laugh. "You've got to be kidding me. You thought you could convince me to go to my death willingly?"

"That's not why I'm here. Rachel is willing to discuss alternatives."

"There are no alternatives. If she wants me back where I belong, then I have to die. If I die, I will be integrated. There will be nothing left of me."

"That's not true."

"You have no idea, Dane. No one does. I'm not even supposed to exist in the first place. Everything from the moment I split from—" I glanced at Enon, realizing this explanation might be a little heavy for such an early acquaintance. He was doing his best to maintain his stoic man-guard appearance, but I could see his eyes narrowing in confusion. No doubt, my connection to hell attracted him, but he didn't need to know I was a branch of the devil. Judging by his risen status, it might be a turnoff. "Look, Dane, I think it's sweet you're trying to keep me from busting up the joint on my way out of here, but I see right through this facade. This is the old you to a tee, and it sickens me."

"The old me?" He frowned.

"You're luring me into a trap with your charms. Go on, Dane, tell me I'm pretty before you kill me." It was a low blow, and I instantly regretted taunting him.

Dane's eyes seemed to darken—in fact, *he* seemed to darken, as if rain clouds had drawn in behind him. "I'm sorry you feel that way, Hennie, but I wasn't sent here to kill you. I was sent here to detain you. The coven will take it from there."

Enon seemed to spark to life at the sound of that. He pushed me aside to face off with Dane. Despite their differing girths, Enon provided an eye-to-eye match-up. "I think that's going to be a little difficult with me around."

Dane looked him over and shook his head. "You really should stay out of this. You are no match for the coven."

Enon chuckled and cracked his neck. "I've been around the block once or twice in the last thousand years. Your little coven doesn't scare me."

Dane narrowed his eyes at the suggestion of the man's age. Since he was technically a demon, I wasn't sure his age should matter, but it did give me pause. It also made me wonder how old *I* was. How far back was the devil's genesis?

"I don't think you've met a coven like this one. Trust me, you won't want to stand in their way. Just like you don't want to be standing in my way right now."

Enon nodded. "You're right. I don't want to be standing in your way. I would rather be standing on your head." Enon's hands curled up like dead spiders. A power grew within his palms. The energy I felt from the dull glow reverberated down to my bones as if I was connected to it—which I suppose I was, since my brand hadn't healed.

Dane looked taken aback. He must not have sensed the demon within him. I wasn't sure what the caveats were for being a risen, but since Enon was the better of the worst, he must not have registered on Dane's evil radar.

Enon's power built up in a matter of seconds. I could feel its strength and I knew he was about to hurt Dane. I didn't want that. I had never wanted anyone to get hurt, but I no longer had the option of being the good guy. The line between good and evil depended on your perspective. It always looked farther away from your side.

Despite my connection to Dane, I resisted the urge to protect him. Maybe one good hit to his ego was what it would take to get him to leave me alone.

Enon's hand jutted out as if he was shoving Dane, but he didn't touch him. The power in his hands burst from him like a bolt of lightning. Conjointly, a boom of thunder shook the walls of the hotel room—or rather it was the ground that had shaken.

I nearly lost my balance, and I was certain my eardrums would start bleeding, but the impact hadn't harmed me.

When I recovered, I looked to see how hurt Dane was, but I didn't have to look far.

He was still there... standing in the doorway as if nothing had happened. His only injury was a small drop of blood escaping one of his nostrils. He reached up and wiped away the blood. He looked at it curiously before turning that same wonderment on Enon. He tipped his head at the man. "That's a good deal of power you're packing, my friend."

Enon stared at him, utterly shocked and pissed. The attack hadn't harmed Dane, but Enon was panting and sweating like he had run a marathon. "What the fuck is going on?" he seethed.

"Let's try this again." Dane stepped into the room, bypassing my old-school protection like they were—well, old-school protection spells. "I'll give you one more warning. Stay out of this."

Dane raised his hands and shoved Enon across the room. He landed against the wall of the bathroom like a wrecking ball, denting the drywall and cracking the 2x4s behind it.

I stared at Dane. I'd been unaware he was capable of such feats of strength. And yet, now that he was inside the room, I could feel power pouring off him like a waterfall. He was using magic. "How?" I asked.

Dane turned to me and raised his chin proudly. "The coven."

"They gave you power?"

"Yes, I'm connected to them now. I'm part of the coven."

"You took my place in the coven?" I whispered. I wasn't sure anything Rachel had done over the last year could compete with this moment. It was on par with... there was nothing to compare it to. They kicked me out and replaced me with a reformed serial killer. It was bad enough that my ex-friend and ex-boyfriend were hunting me down to kill me, but to have them join forces in such an intimate way was a slap in my face.

A wave of prickling heat shattered my control. The betrayal that had inspired my power to be released in the first place was now fueling the anger that was lurking in the background of my mind. I trembled as static electricity circulated over my skin, raising my hair and drawing a look of concern from Dane.

"That bitch!" I yelled and let loose a blast of power that shoved Dane out the door and half-way to the highway.

CHAPTER 13

I STRUTTED ACROSS THE parking lot, eyes blazing with the fires of hell—presumably literally. I could feel the beast clawing at the back of my mind. It wanted out. It wanted vengeance. The problem was, without logic, its revenge would fall upon anything and anyone in its path. I couldn't let it surface. I could never let it surface.

"Hennie, don't do this." Dane scrambled to stand before I could get the upper hand on him.

I fired a warning shot at him—effectively a little bolt of magic to cause him immense pain. It should have hit him and dropped him like a scared puppy, but he waved his hand and the energy returned to me. Instead of dropping him, I had dropped myself. I screamed from the torture I had intended for him.

"We are stronger than ever, Hennie. We will take you back by whatever means necessary."

"*We!*" I screamed. I gritted my teeth against the pain and stood back up. I reached deeper for the full extent of my power to unleash a punishment that would overwhelm the strength of any coven. As the intensity grew inside of me, I found no end in sight.

For a split second, I was looking into the cavernous abyss inside of me—a source of power unrestricted by the laws of physics, nature, or common sense. It was as near to endless as I could comprehend. That thought scared me far more than the danger in front of me. As my anxiety grew, the vigor behind my magical assault shrank.

I looked up at Dane, wide-eyed and ready to confess my concerns about what I saw inside of me. "Dane," I whispered.

"It's okay, Hennie," he whispered. "We can help—"

Enon bowled him over and Dane launched another twenty feet toward a field. "I wasn't using my full strength, asshole," Enon seethed as he stalked after him.

Dane stood up and dusted himself off. "Neither was I." Recognizing that neither of them could triumph purely on the merits of magic, the men resorted to a physical confrontation. They ran forward, crashing into each other with another resounding crack of thunder. Dane had no trouble lifting Enon and slamming him down. The concrete cracked beneath his back. Despite the breath-stealing impact, Enon raised his legs and kicked Dane off him a second later.

With a deft flip-up, Enon was back on his feet and punching Dane in the face. The impact rocked Dane, but he didn't fall. He threw a punch, just as Enon threw his fist again. They hit simultaneously, magical punch for punch. The impact echoed between the buildings, and the men flew away from each other.

The breeze picked up to a bluster, and the clouds rolled in from out of nowhere. I looked to the east and saw a blooming storm. The temperature dropped almost instantly, and real lightning strikes replaced the booming sounds of Dane's and Enon's fists.

The bolts landed in an unnatural formation, one after another, coming closer and closer to me. The last one hit a few hundred yards away from me, threatening to electrocute me.

One by one, my coven arrived, stepping into view as if they had emerged from another dimension. Rachel led the women of the coven in V-formation with Meredith, Ruby, Katherine, and Lynn. They were all dressed in their Clark Kent disguises—robes and habits to hide the true nature of their work. I wasn't sure how the robes of God-fearing women could look ominous to me, but their approach was the equivalent of the four horsemen of the apocalypse. They were beautiful and elegant, but dangerous. Very dangerous.

The storm continued to roil in the background as they took a position in line with one another to face off with me. I turned to do the same. Though I knew I didn't have the intimidation factor, I held an awful lot of power. That was what this was really about.

I had a power that wasn't supposed to be on Earth. I was fucking up the natural order of things. It was nothing new, but now that I had found my internal power source, it was becoming an issue. I wasn't under the devil's thumb anymore. I was autonomous. And that was a problem.

"New boyfriend?" Paul asked from beside me. He was in his usual black suit, looking like a rich pimp. Everything about him screamed *sexy, confident, and in control*. His black hair was combed back to perfection without a single stray hair, even in this wind. His sculpted goatee promised an evil, maniacal laugh at any moment. Even his nails were impeccably manicured. He was beautiful, just like Paula. The fact that they were the same person, two sides to a complicated coin, made my attraction to him more than a little confusing. As if my love life wasn't already a crap shoot.

I looked back at the men punching each other across the field behind us. They weren't likely to kill each other any time soon, so I ignored them. "Where have you been?" I asked Paul, but he had already turned into Paula. The robe and habit she wore as a mockery to God mostly obscured her features, but I knew she had the same dark, glossy hair as Paul. I knew her skin was perfect. Not a single blemish to mar her model-worthy beauty. The fact that she could needle me with her sweet and motherly side was far more irritating to me than the seduction of her handsome counterpart. Probably why she used this image more frequently.

"You know where I've been. I've been waiting for you to come to your senses."

"You couldn't find me, could you?" I flaunted. "And here I thought you were all-powerful."

"Don't get cocky, Hennie," Paula warned, as she usually did when my verbal banter got a little too accurate for her liking. She approached me, but I didn't defend myself. She couldn't technically injure me without hurting my shadow. Violence between us had turned out to be a futile effort in the past, so she had to find new and inventive ways to harm me. And she was good at it.

"This isn't a game anymore. I wasn't lying to you about the impact all of this is having on the world. You've already torn a hole in reality. With every day you fight us, it becomes deeper and deeper."

I sucked in a breath, trying to find an excuse not to believe her. I could detect a lie on anyone—even Paula. She wasn't lying. Still, I held on to the only truth I had left that worked in my favor: God had given me permission to be here. Granted, I had screwed a few things up along the way, but he hadn't evicted me yet.

"You don't want to be responsible for an apocalypse, do you, Hennie?"

"I haven't been using my power. If you bitches would just leave me alone, I could live the rest of my life in peace."

"That's never going to happen!" Rachel called over to me. I turned to her, noting that the coven had linked hands and was quietly chanting under the noise of the wind and thunder. I could feel their presence thickening the surrounding air. "You don't belong in that body. You never have."

"Yes, Hennie, and what of your promise to die?" Paula reminded me. "You agreed to Hennie's request and you can't break that promise. Not without consequences."

"You're right," I said, loud enough for Rachel to hear me. "I did promise to let Hennie die. And she has."

Rachel frowned and glanced at Paula. "What do you mean?"

"I mean, Hennie has left this body. I took a risk—we took a risk. It paid off. She's finally free. She's sitting with the angels now, or at least I'm assuming."

"That's not possible," Rachel snapped at me. The childish snarl on her face weakened her appearance of lorded maturity. She had come a long way in controlling her bitterness, but it still showed through during intense moments. "You can't just take over a body like that."

"I can."

"How?"

"Because I have permission!" My voice echoed between the buildings like the claps of thunder in front of me and the impacts behind me. "When will you believe me? He wants me here."

"You being here is just as much of an abomination as her!" Rachel pointed to Paula.

She shrugged at the accusation as if she had no defense for her blasphemous presence on Earth.

"It has to be that way, doesn't it?" I stepped forward and Rachel tensed. I took more steps, and the women split apart, circling around me so they had me surrounded. To my surprise, Paula took up a position with the circle. She murmured the chant with them. I felt the power envelop me. It was pure, invigorating, and warm, but oppressive. I was standing in the center of a heavenly gauntlet. If I came out the other end unscathed, it was only because they allowed it.

"Has to be what way?" Rachel asked.

I turned back to her and moved close enough so I didn't have to yell to be heard over the storm. "I have to be an aberration. I have to be a mistake. Because if I'm not, then you have no idea what I am. And you can't stand that I have a purpose or a design that you don't know about. You were always envious of my power. Admit it." I was so angry I was spitting into the wind.

Rachel's anger retreated, and she nodded. "You're right, Hennie. I couldn't understand why you, of all people, could be more powerful than me. I hated that I spent my life in service to God and had received nothing for it. Not forgiveness, not peace, and certainly not happiness."

I blinked, surprised that she was willingly throwing her baggage right at my feet. She had apparently overcome the most incapacitating emotion in the human arsenal: shame.

"But I realize now how dangerous power is in the hands of someone who covets more than they deserve. I had to earn the right to hold this power. That's the difference between you and me. That is why you are an aberration. You did not earn the right to be on this Earth—you stole it."

"No," I snapped through gritted teeth. "You're wrong. I stole a body. I never stole the power. The power I possess is my own. It belongs to me like the breath in your lungs belongs to you." I turned to my former coven members, speaking to all of them in turn. "All of you are running under the assumption that I am some evil incarnation like Paula. But I am not. I have no agenda. I am not trying to devastate the Earth. I am trying to live as a human being. I am like..."

Don't say it.

Don't say it.

Don't say it.

"...Christ."

Oh, hell.

"How *dare* you compare yourself to Christ!" Ruby screeched at me before Rachel could spit out the words to denounce my sacrilege.

"No, I just mean because I've come to the Earth in human form to live as a human. I'm not implying sanctity," I backpedaled my way into my doghouse.

"While I'm sure we can argue that point all day, Hennie," Paula jumped in before Rachel could get her words out, "the key difference is that Jesus wasn't exactly packing a nuclear bomb when he walked the Earth."

"The persecution of the innocent will damn the judges!" Kate bellowed out. For a moment, everyone stopped to look at her. I was not unfamiliar with her outbursts, but I wasn't sure if she actually had a purpose in speaking other than to say what was banging around in her head.

After a moment, I turned to Paula. "You're right. This isn't a game anymore. I'm fighting for my life—*my* life. I'm not going to give it up. Not now, not ever."

"We'll see about that," Rachel said behind me. I felt and saw the circle warble around me. The wind stopped and the murmur of chants drowned out the sound of the thunder, though none of the women around me were speaking.

I looked out beyond the circle where Dane and Enon were fighting, but it was only Enon now. He was looking around as if he had lost something. Over toward the motel, I could see people stepping out of their rooms to gawk and point at the unusual storm hovering over the area, adding a downpour of rain that couldn't quite reach the inside of the circle.

Then I found Dane. He had transported into the circle and was standing in line with the others. As I focused on him, I could hear his voice chanting with the others. His lips weren't moving either. They all looked like statues to me.

I could feel the pressure all around me. Their power combined was enormous. The weight of God was forcing me into submission. It hurt, but not physically. I felt the deep cuts of the worst torment a woman could feel—the pain of a friendship torn to shreds for the sake of ego.

I fell to the ground, pressed to the earth with more emotion than I could even understand. I knew what this was. They were using my humanity to their advantage. Just as they had bombarded Dane with the guilt of his actions, they were incapacitating me with my grief. My mother's death, compounded with my father's, and losing Sister Aggie.

And Jess.

My longest and truest friendship. She was dead as well.

The four corners of my foundation, the building blocks that had created the person I am today, were gone. Mother, father, teacher, and friend. The devil had systematically taken them all from me. Carefully enough not to raise my suspicion or trespass on the rules of engagement between realms. Now, I had nothing and no one to depend on.

I was alone.

I heard a banging sound like the echo from inside an aquarium when someone thumps hello to a fish. I could barely move from the weight of my misery, but I turned to see what the noise was. Enon was outside the circle. His heavy fists were beating against the barrier as if it were a snow globe.

He caught my gaze and held it. His lips moved as he spoke, but I couldn't hear him. He lifted his hands and ripped open the collar on his shirt—my shirt.

Damn, I'd liked that blouse.

Enon pressed his hand over the brand on his chest and nodded to me. I raised a shaking hand to my chest and pressed my palm on the mirroring wound. The temporary bond, which would eventually heal and disappear, linked me to Enon. We were essentially a two-person coven.

"Can you feel me?" Enon asked as if he were standing right next to me.

"Yes," I answered.

"I can help you, but I'm too weak. I didn't feed last night." He kneeled down, and though it brought us no closer, I at least didn't have to strain my neck. "You'll share with me. You seem to have plenty of vigor in there. Enough for both of us."

I blinked at him, not sure what sharing meant. I had shared my body with him and that had turned out to be a rather enjoyable experience, but what did it mean to share power? Was it going to come back to bite me in the ass later?

Most definitely, but what choice did I have? The coven was brow-beating me with a heavy hand of sorrow. Unless I turned my emotions off, I was going to submit to them in of a moment of pure suicidal depression.

"What do I do?"

Enon smiled at me. "Just remember last night and let go. I'll take over from there." He leaned in slightly—as much as the barrier allowed. "Don't worry, I'll be gentle this time." He winked at me and I felt a wave of fatigue overcome me, like someone had ripped away my muscles.

Enon sucked in a deep breath and his eyes fluttered with the telltale signs of rapturous pleasure. Since he hadn't made that face last night, I assumed a power rush from me was better than sex. Disappointing and flattering at the same time.

Enon let out a bellowing laugh, then melted into a pile of sand and clothes before my very eyes. For a moment, I thought he had left me, used me for a power rush and run off, leaving me to wither into non-existence. What a dick!

A breeze filled the otherwise still interior of the circle. The concrete before me started to vibrate and disintegrate. Up from the rubble, a dust devil formed, whipping sand in my face as it built itself into a tall pillar.

The pillar gathered more and more earthly matter until it solidified into a form. A man. A naked man. My aforementioned insult now qualified as a compliment.

"Enon?" I asked, and he looked down at me with a childlike grin. This must have been like Christmas morning to him.

"Get up," he commanded. I rose to my feet, though not necessarily by my own volition. I seemed to float. He moved in behind me but kept a small distance between us. "Now, let's show these assholes what we're really made of."

Enon raised his arms and my arms raised. I felt the movements coming from him, but the more we did it, the more in control I felt. I could see I was his puppet, but he was also mine. It was a symbiotic relationship I was unfamiliar with because it was equal. We were, at that moment, like-minded.

It was almost a dance. I swept my hand to the left and Kate screamed in pain. I swept my hand to the right and Ruby yelled out. I raised my hands high and brought them crashing down, and the entire parking lot exploded beneath the feet of the coven, sending them flying in all directions.

The fanning debris of rock and dirt was almost beautiful.

CHAPTER 14

ENON AND I CONTINUED to fight them off one by one. Breaking their concentration as a group may have bought me some time, but that didn't mean each of them wasn't powerful enough to fight on their own.

Rachel arrived with an imprisonment spell that kept me locked in place while Dane attacked Enon again. I heard the smack of a fist, but Enon only laughed at Dane's efforts. I looked back and saw Enon's chest, which appeared to be made of pure rock, had enveloped Dane's fist and wouldn't release him. There were several versions of WTF questions running through my mind, but I wouldn't have time to ask them unless I kept my focus.

I brandished a little strength and bucked off Rachel's spell like snapping a rubber band. Rachel felt the backlash and clenched her teeth in frustration. She really didn't like that I was stronger than her.

Paula, on the other hand, was a different story. She was toting the no-more-games line, and she meant it because the power that struck me was no less painful than all my skin being ripped off. I screamed and dropped to the ground.

"Hang on, Hennie," Enon yelled over the increasingly violent storm around us. The rain, no longer blocked by our magical umbrella, drenched everyone, creating a muddy brawl.

Enon came to me, dragging Dane along with him. He rested his hand on my shoulder, and a trickle of something crawled down my body. At first I thought it was a fungus growing over my skin, but it turned out to be rock. Enon was putting a not-so-metaphysical barrier around me. As it completed its path and relieved my pain, it disappeared.

"You!" Paula yelled. "As soon as I'm done with her, I'm going to put you back in hell."

Enon laughed. "You've been saying that for a century. Go fuck yourself."

"I don't have to. You've been doing it for me." Paula nodded at me.

I could feel Enon tense. I glanced back and saw the confusion on his face, the words not quite matching what he was feeling from me, the truth not making sense even if they did. "Please, don't let go," I whispered. "Just help me get out of here."

Dane broke free of Enon's chest, shattering the surrounding rock as he did. The gaping hole left behind quickly filled in, replaced by flesh. Enon only had seconds to debate his option of continuing the fight before he had to duck another attack from Dane. He pressed his back to mine, and we used my shared power to unleash our double-sided attack.

Meredith and Ruby combined their assault, hitting me high and low. I cast them off with an easy swipe, but as soon as they were gone, Kate and Lynn came at me. Rachel and Paula finally joined forces. Hand in hand, they barreled their linked power into me. The abuse was from heaven and hell alike, humbling me with opposing spectrums of supremacy.

Hatred poured into me in equal measure with love. Together, they turned torrid and deviant. With no balance to grasp onto, the battering magic penetrated my grip on my defenses. I couldn't feel anything beyond the beating of my heart. With every thump, it grew quieter and quieter. This was not a natural death, but under the guise of Rachel's innocence, I knew it would be a legal one. She would take the last hit, ending my existence on Earth and returning me to hell once and for all.

As much as I wanted to be the better person in this situation, I was losing opportunities to escape because I was being too nice. I should have just hit them hard from the very beginning and fled. Now I was once again being overwhelmed. This wasn't the final battle though. I still had one more card to play.

I couldn't.

I shouldn't.

But I had to.

I reached out for the enemy. I reached for the rage that had no heart, no mind, and no soul.

I reached for the beast.

Much as there was a fine line between good and evil, there was an even thinner line between stupidity and genius. And I was about to find out just how thin.

Something lit inside me and, judging by the heat that engulfed me, I presumed it wasn't metaphorical. When I looked back at my attackers, there was a collective gasp. Even Paula looked frightened.

"No," she whispered. "No!" she yelled at me. "You can't! This absolutely can't—"

The fireball I whipped at her head shut her up instantly. She fought back with something similar, but the power dribbled off me. I smiled as she fumed at her impotent power. The beast was much too closely related to her. She couldn't fight her own rage. It would only feed the fire.

"What's happening?" Rachel asked, glancing between us. "What is she doing?"

"The beast," Paula answered. "It's still inside of her. My power is useless against it." She turned to Rachel. "You either finish this now, or the Earth is doomed."

I heard the lie as clearly as a dog could hear a dinner bell. I wanted to call her out on it. To force the truth from her. She obviously knew more about this supposed apocalypse I was going to cause, but she wasn't sharing the specifics. Paula's eyes flickered to me as if she too recognized that she hadn't chosen her words carefully enough.

"Kill her!" Paula screamed, scaring Rachel into action.

And act she did. She threw her hands out, and a visible wave of bright light came at me. I barely had time to react, pushing out my own internal energy as strong as a bomb. I only hoped it was enough to save myself, but not enough to kill Rachel. She may have wanted me dead, but I didn't want her dead. And that wouldn't change, no matter how many times she tried to kill me.

I hoped anyway.

The energies collided and in a brilliant blinding flash of light. The explosion that followed broke the sound barrier and sent everyone flying in all directions.

CHAPTER 15

My vision didn't come back as quickly as my hearing. The reverberation of the explosion was dispersing through the sky like it was echoing up into heaven itself. I didn't have time to question the meaning behind this new complication. Was my power too similar to Rachel's? The beast inside of me was my defense against Paula's power, and now if Rachel couldn't touch me, that should have meant I was free. The only two powerhouses strong enough to even attempt to take me down were useless against me.

If that was true, then why was I being strangled to death? I gasped and choked against the hands wrapped around my neck. I couldn't even feel my body, let alone get the hands off me. I heard laughter in the background, above my own stifled grunts.

"There's always another way to do the same job," Paula said.

I finally blinked away the stars and saw Dane on top of me. He didn't look happy, but that didn't make him any less frightening to me. He shouldn't have been able to kill me. That was against the rules. Dane wasn't an innocent. Or was he?

He was part of the coven now. If he was using their power—God's power—maybe his past didn't matter. He had become their tool. So long as they were innocent, the coven could sanction Dane's actions. Therefore, he could kill this body, sending me back to hell.

Paula appeared over his shoulder. She shook her head at me disapprovingly. "This might just work out for the best."

Rachel was farther back, watching my murder with a shame that made the entire scene that much worse. She looked wrought with grief over having to take my life, but even with tears streaming down her face, she wasn't stepping in to stop it.

I could feel darkness overtaking me, and not the blackout kind. It was not the fiery beast inside of me, either. The hatred blooming inside of me was all mine. I was looking down into the depths of the cavern, kicking rocks over the edge and debating whether I should dive in. I knew what I would find. I knew what was down there. And if I took this flame of anger down to it, then nothing but devastation would come of it.

I wouldn't dare admit the thoughts that were seeping into my brutal imagination as I debated my final step into that gaping darkness. It wouldn't be blood that I would leave in my wake this time. It would be fingernails and eyeballs and… appendages.

Just when I began to formulate the exact method of my revenge, Enon barreled into Dane, knocking him off me.

Enon picked me up and backed away from everyone. I felt my throat open, and I coughed on my first breath of air. He looked around at my potential murderers and rolled his jaw. "What's wrong with all of you?" he yelled in a scolding tone. "I'm the least human among you."

"Not quite," Paula murmured.

Enon locked eyes with her and clenched his jaw. I could feel his magic flare, drawing on the connection between us. He started speaking in a deep voice unfamiliar to me. The words were even less recognizable.

"Don't you dare!" Paula stepped forward, but the earth split right where she intended to step. She moved positions in a flash behind us, but the earth split there too. Every step she took to reach us only caused another fracture in the ground. She screamed in frustration. When she caught my eye, she gave me a loathsome glare. "I will find you!"

Rachel and the others tried to reach me as well. They bounded over the rifts like free-jumping enthusiasts, but every momentous leap only took them farther away as the ground rolled away from us like waves.

"Hennie!" Dane made one last attempt to reach me, but I was already sinking into the earth with Enon. I looked around at the quicksand enveloping us.

"What's happening?" I whispered.

Enon turned to me and gave me a cocksure smile. "Hold your breath."

Then we went under.

CHAPTER 16

F ROM ONE SUFFOCATION TO another, the pressure of the earth was all around me. There was no sign of up or down. There was no hope of swimming to the surface, either. The ground had cemented in place like a statue. I knew someday I would be dead and buried, but I had hoped it would come in that order.

When there was no air left, and I started to panic, the surrounding ground shook. The steady vibration shook the soil down, even as the dirt beneath me pushed upward. After a moment, the world broke open for me. I emerged from the earth, as useless and scared as the day I was born.

Enon seemed to come out of nowhere and wrap around me. He hugged me close while I cried a few long-overdue tears paired with a few new ones.

When I was calm enough to look at my surroundings, I realized I was in a cemetery. I had just crawled from the grave like a zombie. The only difference was, it wasn't my plot. I looked at the name on the marker. Edna Thorpe. "Where are we?" I asked.

"Safe. That's all that matters."

"How did we get here?" I knew we had transported, but since he had made such an issue about not being able to do it, I wondered what had changed.

"It's easy for me to move around when I have the strength. Moving you with me, however, is a whole other issue. Luckily, you seem to have access to an endless fountain of energy."

I rolled over to look at him. As I'd suspected, he had meant the comment to sound overtly sexual. "Why did I have to be in the dirt?"

He shrugged. "It's just how I do it. Maybe next time you can click your heels together."

"I've never done that before."

"You did it last night."

"I don't remember how."

"The way you do everything in magic: with intent. Do you even understand how powerful you are?"

"Yes," I admitted dolefully.

"You sound tormented by it."

"Enon, I have... I am..." I paused, not wanting to speak.

Enon shifted onto his hands and looked down at me. "What is it?"

"I'm a fragment of hell's trinity. Paula is the devil's human form. She's joined forces with my former coven and ex-boyfriend to kill me because I shouldn't exist. And according to her, I'm going to cause the apocalypse or something like that. You should get as far away from me as you can."

Enon thought about that for a moment, even as he looked over my body hungrily. "What do you mean by a fragment?"

I took a breath and chose my words carefully. "Paula is the ram. The beast is a representation of his anger. The serpent—the part of him I come from—is his mind."

"Mind, body, and… heart?" Enon debated the designation, but the metaphor worked as well as any other I had used to explain my overly complex alter egos. His eyes flickered over mine as if he were figuring something out. "That's how you were able to stay." He raised his hand to my forehead. "Mind." He grazed his finger along my throat before pressing his palm into the cleft between my breasts. "Heart." He dragged his hand lower to my stomach. "Body." For a moment, I thought he might go lower, but instead, he moved his hand back up and traced a cross on my forehead. "Soul," he whispered.

I took in a stuttered breath, waiting for the drama to begin, but he just watched me, watching him. After several seconds a silence, I cleared my throat. "Did you hear the part about me causing the apocalypse?"

Enon scoffed. "Ah, God, you're so young. I guess that makes sense. You had to start from scratch. Although I'm willing to bet, you have the instincts required to drive these powers properly. We just have to unlock them."

"I don't want to drive this car. I want to put it in park, turn off the engine and walk away slowly so I don't start the rapture."

Enon laughed and stood up. "Do you know how many apocalypses I've lived through? At least a dozen. Guess how many successful ones?" Enon reached down. I took his hand, and he pulled me upright. I noticed he had found some new clothing along the way. Since the polo and slacks looked rather nice, I couldn't help but worry that perhaps someone had been buried in them—or at least they had until today. "None," he answered his own quiz. "All an apocalypse means is that mankind is in some kind of danger. Hell, half the time they do it to themselves."

"Themselves? If the human race had been through a dozen apocalypses, I would have heard something about it."

Enon raised his hands to my cheeks and gently squished them. "You are so cute when you have no idea what you're talking about," he gushed.

"Stop it!" I slapped his hands away. "Don't condescend. Just answer me."

"We can talk about that later. First, I need to introduce you to some people." Enon tugged me along by my hand.

"What? Who?" I tried to pull back on his hand, but he was much too heavy for me to stop without using my power, a move I knew would be especially stupid after my recent near-death experience.

"Some... well, I wouldn't call them friends. Frankly, they're idiots, but they are the best we have to work with at the moment."

"To work with?" I asked, still searching for the details Enon liked to leave out of every conversation. "Who am I working with?"

He turned back and gave me a crooked grin. "Your new coven."

CHAPTER 17

"H EY, ENON!" I WATCHED the twenty-going-on-fifteen goth girl bound across the wine cellar and meet Enon at the bottom of the stairs. She jumped into his arms and gave him a nasty, wet kiss, which he didn't pull away from. I waited patiently a few steps up while she practically humped his leg. When she finally pulled her suckerfish lips off him, she looked directly at me.

She had the usual black hair and endless eye makeup. Her lower lip held three piercings, which made me curious about the comfort of her kisses. She wore a long black gown with tattered sleeves like Elvira. Beneath that she had light blue denim pants and heavy black army boots with an excess of buckles.

A year ago, her glare might have annoyed me. And if I had known Enon for more than one night, I might have been jealous of her display. However, as it stood, I found everything about her to be fake. Fake face, fake attitude, and fake blood-red nails.

A smile curved on my lips, but it contradicted the very nature of smiles. It was as much a threat as congeniality. I didn't care who she was, or whom she fucked, but she needed to get out of my face. The young woman seemed to sense I was not in the mood for a catfight and retreated from Enon. She ran over to the rest of what was presumably my new coven.

I leaned forward and whispered in Enon's ear, "Please tell me that's not my competition."

He chuckled softly. "Don't worry. Like I told you, humans don't really do it for me. She just really likes sucking my cock, and when I have nothing better to do, I let her."

"And I thought human men were pigs."

"If she's making you jealous, I could fuck you right here on the stairs, so she knows I'm yours." He looked back at me, not even remotely kidding.

Aside from concerns about splinters, the amount of dirt still crusted on me from my dirt bath, and my general displeasure with public nudity, I couldn't help wondering when Enon had become *mine*. My one-night stand had turned into a beneficial short-term arrangement and now, over the horizon, I was seeing a long-term commitment. As useful as he was turning out to be, I couldn't get Dane out of my head. He had been so angry when he saw me with Enon and yet when it came time for the coven to kill me; he had been the weapon of choice. There was anguish in his eyes, but not enough to stop him from squeezing my life away.

"Well?" Enon persisted. "Get on all-fours then."

I suddenly realized he would actually do as he threatened and I wrinkled my nose at him. "No! Freak! I just mean she's like a teenager. I would have thought you had better taste than that."

Enon shrugged dismissively. "Everyone's a teenager to me."

I grabbed his shoulder before he could walk away. "Are you really a thousand years old?" I whispered in his ear.

He nodded. "Don't worry, the memories fade so fast. I'm basically like a really old man."

"Old?"

"Two or three hundred years old."

"Oh, good," I said flatly. "And here I was afraid we would have nothing in common."

Enon drew back and stepped up on a higher tread to meet me eye to eye. "Maybe I need to prove something to you on these steps." I frowned, legitimately concerned he wouldn't let the staircase sex drop, but he smirked and drew away the moment I revealed my fear.

"Everyone, this is Hennie," Enon announced as he joined the group at the industrial wire spool table on the far end of the wine cellar. Everyone looked up at me: the goth girl and three other men. There was the vampire-wannabe guy, the Dungeons & Dragons aficionado, and by all standards of snap judgments, the former-military anarchist. "Hennie, this is Raven." Enon pointed to the goth girl, and I nearly snorted out loud at the predictable name.

"Vlad." He pointed to the vampire guy, and I did snort at that one. Aside from his pale skin, which came naturally to him, he was further pushed into paler by his long-sleeved black turtleneck shirt. However, instead of the conventional black hair, Vlad was donning a dark red mop of sloppy locks. It matched the bright red medallion hanging from his neck. When he locked eyes with me, he gave me a lopsided smile. I was certain he intended it to be a snarl, so he could show off his elongated canines, which didn't appear to be plastic. He must have had a very flexible dental plan.

"Merlin." Enon motioned to the next young man.

"Oh, actually, I changed it to Puck," the geeky guy corrected him. He was the least goth among them. In fact, his tight brown curls and acne-prone face belonged in a high school locker room, being tormented by jocks rather than here. Then again, perhaps that was why he was here. I could hardly blame him for that. I hadn't enjoyed high school either. Only politicians and sadists ever enjoy high school. "I thought Merlin was too civil disobedience, whereas Puck was more like intrigue and deception. What do you think?" Puck asked eagerly.

"I love it," Enon said.

Puck sat back with a contented smile, as if Enon's approval had meant everything to him. I kept my eyes on the boy. When his gaze finally flickered over to me, his contentment evaporated. He tried to put on a fake smile before his eyes drifted to his lap.

"And finally, this is our master of ceremonies, Zeus."

Zeus turned to me and bowed his head like he was sitting in a stately court and not in an old basement with his feet propped up on furnishings of questionable quality. The old green fatigues he was wearing didn't belong to him. He was too young to know the atrocities of Vietnam or Korea, though I sensed he would argue his grandfather did so he could justify wearing them as fashion. His shaven blond hair reminded me of Dane—or at least how he used to wear it. Zeus even had those same beautiful blue eyes, made brighter against the backdrop of smeared black eyeliner. Looking at him, being reminded of Dane, made my stomach lurch. That knife had already been inserted and twisted more than once, but somehow the wound was still fresh, ready and waiting for every drop of lemon juice I could happen upon.

This time, I couldn't hold my intimidating gaze. I dropped my stare and took a calming breath so I didn't erupt into tears—or start something on fire. Either was just as likely these days.

I was past the point of being amused by this ramshackle group of misfits. This endeavor was a waste of my time. It annoyed me that Enon thought this goth squad could save my life. I may have been a little undertrained in magic, and I may not have had 300 years' worth of knowledge, but I knew hacks when I saw them. I wasn't about to defend myself against the scourge of hell with a group that had barely recovered from puberty.

I turned to Enon and leveled a perturbed glare at him. "I'm done." I walked away, ready to go my own way if that's what I had to do. It wouldn't be the first time. At least this time *I* was the one doing the leaving. There was some pride to be had in that.

"Zeus," Enon said. "Show her what we can do."

"Just forget it, Enon." I reached the stairs, but Enon grabbed my shoulder and dragged me to a stop.

"Hennie, wait, please, just listen." I reluctantly turned back to listen to what he had to say. "Look, I know they are a rag-tag group, but with my help, they've come a long way."

"A long way to what?" I dropped a step to face him. "We are well past the Ouija board stage on this one," I said, a little quieter.

"I know," Enon agreed.

"I seriously doubt anyone in this room is going to be ready to fight the devil on my behalf." Enon's face flickered with doubt, proving my point. "I appreciate everything you've done for me, but I'm not going to put these kids in the path of hell. I'll figure this out for myself. Or die trying," I mumbled bitterly and turned away.

"How disappointing," Enon said dismissively. I drew back and propped my hands on my hips.

"What is *that* supposed to mean?"

He looked me over with more contempt than I thought I deserved. "You're ready to face the evils of hell, but you can't lower yourself to ask for help."

"I'm not being egotistical, Enon. I'm being realistic. I don't want them to get hurt."

"Neither do I." Enon's eyes danced over me again. This time, there was more warmth in them. "But I don't want you to get hurt, either. At the very least, stay a while. We'll keep you hidden." He reached up and tugged on the crooked collar of my shirt. "You look like you need a break... and a shower." He smirked at me and I rolled my eyes. "Why don't you give my way a chance? Please," he added.

I took a breath and nodded. "Fine, I'll see what they can do before I storm out."

"Thank you. I'll make it worth your time, I promise."

I detected a hint of intrigue in his voice and I smiled at him. "Is that so?" I whispered and came in closer. I leaned in and kissed him. I should have been above flaunting my relationship with Enon in front of his side piece, but I decided she should know who was going to win this competition right now, so we could skip the hair-pulling and go straight to being mortal enemies.

Enon stiffened, surprised that I had chosen to pee on his leg. It didn't take long for him to give in, though. He wrapped his arm around me and pulled me closer. The kiss went on longer than it should have. His tongue dipped into my mouth, calling to my desires in a way that made me wonder if the stair-sex was still on the table.

Peals of laughter finally broke us apart. I opened my eyes, and for a moment, I saw Dane staring back at me. Blue eyes, buzz cut, and... too much black eyeliner.

Zeus licked his lips and backed away from me. "Not bad, Enon. She kind of tastes like dirt right now, though."

"What?" I frowned at Zeus, searching for some explanation for why he was standing in front of me and not Enon. He shifted out of my line of sight, revealing Vlad, Puck, Raven, and Enon sitting at the spool table behind us. They were all laughing at my expense—though Enon seemed to try to contain himself.

I looked back at Zeus, realizing the entire conversation had been with him. He had disguised himself as Enon. He restrained his smirk, and he looked a little guilty, but he was nonetheless very pleased with his successful trickery. I, however, was a little pissed about the deception, so I slapped him across the face.

He took the hit like a beaten dog, not even backing away when my snarling face threatened to do it again.

"Easy, Hennie." Enon ran over to intercept me before I could do more damage. "Take your anger out on me, not him."

As requested, I punched him in the gut, but he didn't flinch at the impact. Punching him was a lot like punching a wall. Satisfying, but only for a second.

"The thing is, Hennie, we all have to hide our abilities—much like your former coven. Except instead of joining a convent, we are, well—"

"Rejects," Puck contributed the word like a medal of honor, but the look on his face said the formerly weaponized word still had some sting to it.

"In plain sight is the best way to hide real magic," Enon continued. "I was in a band during the sixties that was a cover for a rather powerful coven. I met a lot of groovy people and hunted down a shitload of demons." Enon's eyes glazed for a moment. "Those were good times."

I grimaced at his reverie and crossed my arms. He was like a vampire exorcist. A vampicist. An exorpire. No, never mind.

"Come meet the group properly." Enon ushered me back to the table and sat me down on one of the squat barrels around it. Zeus carefully scooted around me and took the back chair so he could lean against the wall. I caught his eye to glare at him, but the look he sent back to me wasn't what I'd thought it would be. He was definitely afraid I was still going to retaliate for the indiscretion, but he held my gaze with wary anticipation, as if he would gladly take any attention from me—even if it was another slap. Beaten dog indeed.

"Let's try this again." Enon moved behind Raven and put his hands on her shoulders. I pretended not to care, but I was tracking all ten of his fingers with a vengeance. Raven gave me a smug smile before resting her cheek against one of his hands. Again, I reminded myself that I had no claims to Enon. I had no claims to anyone, even though everyone had claims on me.

"You aren't seriously going to join these idiots, are you?" my shadow asked from the reflection in the wine bottle in front of me. "Can't you see he's just using you? He's been alive for a thousand years. Think of how many girlfriends he's had and lost to human death. Do you really think a man so old can be loyal to anyone?"

I grabbed the bottle off the table and flung it behind me. Somewhere near the stairs, it shattered. Everyone looked back at it, then at me. The perplexed looks on their faces were not as much worry as simply shock.

"That was a $300 bottle of wine," Vlad said with a note of disappointment in his voice.

"Sorry," I murmured, not wanting to explain my shadow. I was already a freak among weirdos. I didn't want to risk sinking to the level of a *creepy* freak. Not that randomly breaking reflective surfaces had helped my reputation in the past. "Where were we?"

"I was about to tell you about Raven," Enon said, not giving the broken bottle another glance. "I know your former coven relies on traditional symbiotic rituals, but I've never found that to be as effective as focused training." Enon moved to the cache of wine behind the table and grabbed a dusty bottle. He popped the cork with a quick movement I couldn't quite follow. He poured a glass of wine for himself and Vlad before offering some to me. I declined since I knew my shadow would just show up in the wine's reflection.

"Certain people tend to lean toward certain skills. Zeus, as you saw, is good at disguising his image. With some concentration, he can even do it for other people." I looked at Zeus to confirm this, but he looked away this time. "Now Raven, well, she is very special. Aren't you?" Enon looked at her proudly and she practically melted into the barrel she was sitting on. I almost felt bad for her at that moment. There was nothing worse than being consumed by love. Unrequited or not, it was still sad to see. "Why don't you show her?"

Raven nodded and turned to face me. She looked at me intensely. She wasn't mad, just very... stare-y. I held her gaze, if only to see what she would do next. "Have some wine," she said.

"No, thanks."

"Have some wine."

I sighed, seeing that playing this game would be required. "Okay." I took a drink from the glass someone had put in front of me. It was a little fruitier than expected, but like most red wines, it was much too dry. When I turned back, Raven was beaming. "What?" I asked. "You convinced me to drink some wine I didn't even want, so what?"

"What wine?" she asked.

"This wine." I pointed to the glass in front of me, still half-full of wine.

Raven laughed and Puck joined in. "That is so awesome," he said, reaching past Vlad for a high five. Since Raven didn't look at him, she missed the invitation. Puck put his hand down, letting the potential for camaraderie die along with his spirits.

"There is no wine in front of you, Hennie," Enon explained.

I picked up the glass of wine and showed it to him. "This isn't here?"

"Nope," Puck answered and snickered.

"This won't do anything." I threw the wine in Puck's face. From my perspective, the red liquid splattered all over his face and clothes, but he didn't flinch when it hit him. Everyone had a good laugh at that.

I stared at the glass in my hand, which still contained the same amount of wine I had started with. I closed my grip around it and watched it shatter in my grip. The shards made me bleed as they should, but there was no pain. The blood was no more real than the wine. I blinked away the vision, forcing myself to see the truth.

"I make people see what I want," Raven said.

"Isn't that kind of the same thing Zeus does?" I asked.

"No, it's completely different," she defended, as if it wasn't the first time she had needed to.

"Zeus affects the external. Changes the way things look in real-time for everyone. Raven changes the mind of the individual," Enon explained. "We didn't see the wine. Only you."

"So, like Zeus, but less effective."

"I'm effective!" Raven looked to Enon, desperate for his guidance. When he didn't immediately cajole her, she turned back to me, a determined focus in her eyes. "Spiders!" she yelled at me.

Even as the word escaped her lips, I felt dozens and then hundreds of creepy crawly things making their way up my legs. I jumped at the sight of them burrowing beneath my shirt and popping back out of my cleavage. It was a little more impressive than imaginary wine, but it also pissed me off.

I ignored the tickle of the bugs on my skin and gave her my best don't-fuck-with-me look. "Cut." The word escaped my mouth before I could stop myself.

Raven's pale white cheek exploded as if an invisible knife had slashed her. She yelped and reached for her cheek. When she saw the blood, she wailed and held her hand out to Enon. "Is this real?"

"Yes, it's real," I answered and leaned in closer to her. "My power isn't make-believe."

"Hennie," Enon scolded me and pressed his hand to Raven's cheek to staunch the blood.

I leaned back, knowing I had taken it too far—again. The spiders disappeared as Raven's concentration went to her injury. "I'm not impressed, Enon," I said callously. "When do you show me something I can use?"

Vlad reached over to Raven's cheek. Enon backed his hand away. I watched the deep rent heal beneath his touch. The display silenced her drama and drew a look of reverence from her. "Thank you, Vlad."

Vlad nodded and turned a stony glare on me. He didn't seem to be afraid of me like the others. As a healer, he probably didn't fear many things. With the threat of pain gone, the only thing left to fear was death. "That's my power," he stated arrogantly.

"All right, well, that is a legitimately useful power," I admitted. "Is that all you can do?"

"Yeah—I mean no, but—"

"What about you, Puck? What's your contribution?"

Puck looked around as if he hadn't realized the show and tell was eventually going to come to him. "Oh, ah..." He leaned across the table, reaching his hand toward me. I shifted back out of his reach.

"Just tell me what you do."

"Oh, right, well, I can freeze people. If I concentrate really hard, I can freeze an entire room. I used to think I was freezing time, but it turned out to be—"

"Great, thanks." I looked at Enon. "Are you serious? This isn't a coven. This is the makings of a supernatural heist."

"Well, yeah," Puck said with a scoff.

"Puck." Enon stared at him with wide eyes.

I glanced between the men. "You mean that's what you actually are?" I asked Puck.

He glanced at Enon but he didn't seem to recognize the social cue for *shut the fuck up*. "Enon needs to hunt demons, so we help him with that. And when we are in need of a little cash, he helps us with a job."

My mouth dropped open, unable to prevent the ridiculous stuttered guffaws that were escaping. "You're bank robbers!" I stood up, knocking over my barrel seat.

"That doesn't mean they can't help you," Enon said.

"I think it really does."

"They are strong enough. They just haven't had to use their skills for more altruistic purposes yet."

"Altruistic?" The word incensed me, increasing my volume more than necessary. "We aren't saving the goddamn whales, Enon! I'm being hunted by a former serial killer, a powerful coven, and the devil incarnate. I can't be dicking around with amateurs."

"Wait, you were serious about that?" Zeus asked. "The real devil? The real-real devil?"

I turned to him. "Yeah, Zeus, the one with the horns."

"Whoa, Enon, man, I don't know about that." Zeus looked at him with worry.

"Yeah, we can't fight *Satan*," Raven complained.

"You don't have to fight him. Hennie will. This is about making her stronger."

"No," I said flatly, and turned my attention back to him. "This is about making *you* stronger. You want more power so you can get more demons like you did in the sixties." I walked away.

"Is that what your imaginary friend told you?" Enon asked.

I stopped with one foot on the first step. I wanted to know how he knew about him. Could he see him as Dane could? I resisted the urge to ask, though. It didn't matter. I continued up the stairs while his clansmen barraged Enon with worried questions.

Chapter 18

I stepped out of the tavern to find the sun dipping toward the horizon. I tried to place myself, but all I could surmise was that I was farther east than I had been. I was in a city, but not a big one, judging by its cleanliness.

I passed through the brick columns leading to the sidewalk and turned right. Left would take me back to the cemetery, but I wasn't interested in another dirt nap. I needed to find a hotel for a proper shower and possibly a drink.

I passed by a small park surrounded by tall black iron fencing. The rustle of running water drew my attention, so I slipped inside. Beyond a mess of green plants that begged to be weeded, I found a large koi pond. The fish eagerly popped to the surface, effectively begging me for food. Judging by their size, someone fed them regularly.

"Scatter." I splayed my fingers, facilitating their departure.

After a minute or two, the water settled and offered me a perfect mirror to gaze into. I bolstered my courage and peered down at myself. "Okay." I resented the level of defeat I could hear in my voice. "Tell me what I don't want to hear."

My shadow came into view as if he had arrived behind me. "I've been trying to tell you for six months," he said, perturbed.

"I know," I said.

"Broken mirrors, scratched chrome, greasy glass—"

"I'm listening now!" I snapped. "I heard a lie from Paula. I can't tell where the exaggeration veers from the truth."

"And what makes you think I will clarify if she won't?"

"Because you're different. You're me. Or you were once. Or I was once." My shadow perked his brow, mildly impressed by my acceptance of our link. "Just tell me this: why does the devil care about stopping the apocalypse? If I'm unraveling the laws of physics, isn't that the type of chaos the devil might enjoy watching?"

My shadow chuckled and sat down on the edge of the pond with me. I could feel his heat next to me, but it was only the reflection I could see. "Paula isn't acting on behalf of humanity. She's acting on her own behalf. She is, after all, human. She isn't worried about the tear that will bring down humanity. She's worried about what God will do to fix it."

"What will He do to fix it?"

"Put us back together."

I frowned. "Isn't that what she wants? Isn't that what she has always wanted?"

"No, I mean He will put *all* of us back together. Including her."

I scoffed and looked out into the garden. I could smell roses, but I couldn't see them. There were several honey bees floating over the funnel-shaped flowers in the bed across from me. They would dip in and out, pick a new flower seemingly at random, and repeat. "She doesn't want to leave either. She wants me to fix the tear before God has to get involved."

"I thought it was a genius idea for her to contact your body's soul. Implanting the beast brought the original Hennie to the surface like a proper possession—only in reverse. And the promise." My shadow contemplated that. "We almost had you, but you were a little too strong. Congratulations, by the way, on using Enon to your advantage. What are the chances that you would meet a risen just in the nick of time?" He asked conspiratorially, but I ignored him. I had questions of my own that needed answers.

"What is he exactly?"

"Some would call him a golem, but risen is the preferred name. He isn't a possession or an assimilation. He's a very powerful demon."

"How powerful?"

"Powerful enough to cross realms. Powerful enough to escape hell and form a body from the earth."

"He's made of dirt?"

"I'm sure if we were speaking in terms of science, I would say he is created by matter manipulation. He simply uses the earth for his base material. Fortunately, holding his form is an exhaustive use of his power, otherwise he might be more of a nuisance to humanity. That's why he needs to feed on other demons. He draws out their energy and uses it to recharge himself. That's why he is so keen on you. You are an absolute goldmine to him." My shadow leaned in to whisper seductively. "The first soul to ever exist. He could live off you alone for decades upon decades. It's a match made in hell, if you ask me."

"What about the beast?"

"That's another problem altogether." He leaned back, speaking with disdain. "There is a reason I split myself. My rage was becoming a hindrance. Blind hatred, while invigorating, made life cumbersome. Much like my conscience was a thorn in my side—" My shadow nodded to me. "—the beast also prevented me from acting rationally. I placed my desires in Paula, my anger in the beast, and that left me to think without regard to emotions or physical entrapments. Unfortunately, it also left me alone with you."

"You must have been thrilled when I left. No longer having to abide by my moralities..."

"Is that how you think this works?" my shadow asked with a hint of menace in his tone. He raised his hand and stroked my cheek. I felt a tingle where the contact would be if he weren't merely a figment. "Do you think I don't feel you, because we can't touch?" He leaned forward to whisper again. "Did you really think your pain is all I am subjected to? I feel *everything* you feel, Hennie. I feel your hunger, your anxiety, your loneliness. Your morality and sanctimonious opinions are still inside of me. Every new experience you have belongs to me as much as you. We're on this little adventure together. Always have been."

I swallowed, thinking about the many times I had felt alone and never truly been alone. "If we're on this journey together and you feel what I feel, you must sense how strongly I want to stay."

My shadow rolled his jaw. "Yes."

I looked down at him in the water, and he looked back at me. "That's why Paula hasn't been able to locate me, isn't it?" My shadow looked furious, but he didn't deny it. "You won't tell her where I am? You won't help her. That's why she's been waiting for the coven to pick up on my magic. You're protecting me."

"Don't confuse apathy for empathy!" my shadow scolded in a harsh voice that sounded like it should have belonged to the beast.

"This must be so frustrating for you," I said with never-before-seen sympathy. "I do belong to you." My shadow's eyes returned to mine, alerted to anything resembling submission. "I understand that now. I'm not quite the fragment I purported to be, though. I'm still inside of you. I've just reached out. Crossed the barrier of two realities to be part of something real. And I've taken you with me. Forced you to view the world with unbiased eyes. It's because I don't remember being you that I can see humanity without a bitter grudge. I've shown you something that in millennia you never would have found in hell. I showed you—"

"Oh, please, don't say what I think you are about to say," my shadow threatened.

"Love," I finished.

My shadow hissed and stood up. He walked away and for a moment I thought he wouldn't come back, but eventually he did. He sat back down, as close to me as he could. He stroked my hair while his words susurrated at every opportunity. They tickled my ear as if a tiny forked tongue was coming out of his mouth.

"You, sweet girl, have no idea what love is. Do you think the beast was born from nothing? Do you think such an intense hatred could be grown from my ego alone? No, no, no, Hennie. That anger... The anger that now sits inside of you, waiting to force its way to the surface, is what love looks like when it's left to sour over the course of centuries. So don't pretend you've introduced me to the ways of the heart. I was the first to feel His love. And I was the first to feel His wrath. That is what the beast is, Hennie. Heartbreak."

My shadow thankfully slipped away and disappeared so I could jam my finger in my ear and lessen the itch his hissing words had left me. "Remind me never to give the devil love advice," I mumbled to myself before heading out of the garden.

I at least had a few more answers. Not that I could depend on the loyalty of my other self, but for the time being, he wasn't ratting me out. That meant the coven would have to track me down with Rachel's magic and Dane's instincts alone. They were more than capable of finding me, but if I kept my magical usage to a minimum, I would be okay... for a while.

CHAPTER 19

I RAN INTO ENON outside the garden. He was leaning against the brick pillars waiting for me. I stopped in front of him and looked over his body perfunctorily. "Are you really a golem?" I asked.

His eye twitched, and he shook his head. "Golem is a dirty word." He raised his palm, and the skin swelled. What first looked like a boil turned into a mound of sand. Then that sand formed into an apple before my very eyes. He tossed it to me to examine. The peel, while much too red to be advertised as delicious, was smooth and almost shiny. It looked and felt like an apple. "Taste it," he said.

I snorted. "Quote every villain ever."

"Go on, Hennie. This isn't Eden. Take a bite."

I raised the apple to my lips and glanced around before taking a bite. I chewed the sweet flesh carefully, waiting for it to turn to ash in my mouth or for a worm to burrow out of the core. Enon watched me and waited for me to swallow my bite before shifting away from the brick column. He circled behind me. "The Earth provides many pleasures. We feast from her every day. Drinking her, breathing her, and tasting her. You may think of me as an extension of her."

I pushed away the imagery of having sex with a mound of dirt, reminding myself that matter manipulation was probably a more accurate term. "How powerful are you?" I turned to face Enon, and he smiled unabashedly.

"Hmm, let's see if I can describe it."

"Not as strong as the devil."

"No, not that strong, but strong enough to rip a soul out of you. Strong enough to support a coven of laymen. And strong enough to put a few dents into your demon hunter." I winced at the mention of Dane. Seeing him again was reminding me what I had lost—not just our relationship, but a chance at a semi-normal life. Enon noted the movement and raised his palm, placing it over the brand on my chest. "I can make that pain disappear."

Our connection strengthened, and I felt overwhelmed by the same desire that had initially led me to sleep with him. As much as I had enjoyed that night, I didn't think wallowing in carnal pleasures was going to help my situation any. I drew away from his touch before my body could override my mind. He didn't seem hurt by my rejection, just amused.

"How about you help me make this mess disappear first?" I motioned to the condition of my clothes.

He chuckled. "Fair enough. I have an apartment over the tavern. You can clean up there."

Twenty minutes later, I found myself a good deal cleaner, but I hadn't been able to resist Enon when he joined me behind the shower curtain. Pressed to the wall and wrapped around him, I could only surrender to the pleasure he provided me.

Somewhere in the back of my mind, I knew my connection to him was a bad idea, but my overlapping climaxes made it difficult to recognize the danger right in front of me. The strange thing was, I didn't feel any negative or positive energy from him when we were together. With Dane, I had always felt a tinge of darkness. Presumably, that was what allowed him to see demons. When connected to the coven, I felt their goodness.

However, Enon felt empty. Was that what a risen was? Was he nullified by the earth? Or was he powerful enough to hide his true self from me? Was this just another heist? If so, what did he intend to steal from me?

CHAPTER 20

"YOU HAVE TO RELAX," Enon said as he circled around the coven. It wasn't the first time he had said it and I was getting sick of hearing it.

"Easy for you to say," I grumbled. "You aren't being molested by four strangers."

"We aren't going to molest you," Vlad said disgustedly. He was holding down my left leg. He shifted his left hand closer to my knee. In case his proximity to my crotch might have caused my comment.

"There has to be some representation of surrender," Enon said. "Do you want to do this naked?"

"No," Puck answered. He looked at me with a terrified expression on his face. He squeezed my left arm as if begging me not to say yes. I imagined he had taken his fair share of teenage torment care of a boy's locker room.

"Don't worry, Puck," I said. "No one is taking their clothes off. Why can't I just agree to the link, as I did with you?"

"You and I are already connected by a similar power. Humans have no such link with each other. That's why magic requires so many daunting and irritating rituals. We have to bypass the natural laws, and for humans, that takes more than intention." I could tell Enon was getting annoyed I wasn't cooperating, but with so many doubts on my mind, I couldn't find the focus I needed to complete the connection to my new coven. And really, I didn't want a new coven. I wanted my old one. I wanted something familiar and comfortable.

"You can do this, Hennie." The words were from Zeus, but he had changed forms. Instead of the black-eyed soldier holding down my right arm, it was... my father.

I nearly bucked all four of them off me, but Vlad and Raven jumped on my legs, pressing their hands and knees painfully into my shins.

"How the fuck did you get his face?" I spat the words at him.

"I showed him," Enon admitted.

"You take him off right now, you bastard!"

"It's okay, Hennie." The sweet words came from my left. Puck was gone, replaced by my mother. I knew this was still Zeus, pushing his power onto Puck, but the vision brought tears to my eyes.

"No!" I screamed and bucked again and again, but my physical strength was waning as the emotions rose into my throat. "Stop it!"

"You're not alone anymore, Hennie." I looked up and saw Sister Aggie circling me now instead of Enon. There was no way to tell if this was still Zeus or if Enon had manipulated his own form. Regardless, the face of my former mentor was twisting my emotions that much more. Tears poured from my eyes and I started to hyperventilate. Instead of feeling trapped by their grips, I was being pressed down by my grief.

My desperation to connect was taking the front row, and I was relinquishing my grip on my power. I was ready to merge. I was prepared to bare my soul.

"That's right, Hennie." I looked down at the familiar voice and face that had taken over Raven. I should have been glad to see Jess. She should have poured just as much grief into my veins, but she didn't. Just looking at her face reminded me of the beast inside of me. The beast that had killed her. Instead of drawing on my loneliness and guilt and grief as the others did, Jess's face brought out my anger.

"No!" I screamed, and a rush of power surged inside of me like a gas cloud igniting.

The explosion interrupted my quartering and propelled the coven in all directions. They hit the walls and wine racks, making the bottles jingle. Enon was the only one left standing after the display. His ire was stone cold as he looked at me, panting from my exertion. He didn't take his eyes off me as he motioned everyone back in. "Again," he said with determination. The coven reluctantly followed his instructions and limped back over for another round of my abuse-laden stubbornness.

CHAPTER 21

I WATCHED VLAD HEALING Puck's broken arm with as much disinterest as I could muster. I wanted to apologize for hurting him. Technically, it had been the staircase railing that had broken his arm; I was just the asshole who had thrown him into it.

Vlad was giving me another dose of his disapproval. He must have been a rather sympathetic person for healing to come so easily to him.

"Again," I heard Enon announce.

"Are you kidding me?" I asked before any of his crew could put up a fight. "A broken wrist." I motioned to Raven. "A broken arm." I motioned to Puck. "And untold concussions? I think we're done for today."

"We're done when you surrender." Enon propped his hands on his hips. I could feel his power flagging through our mutual bond. It made the burn on my chest itch.

I pursed my lips and narrowed my eyes at him. Perhaps it was time for me to test my new "boyfriend's" limits. I propped my hands on my hips, mirroring him. "Kneel." The word was quiet, but it was a crushing weight that dropped him instantly to the floor. And I thought he had been glaring at me before.

"Lips." The mere mention of them and they clamped together, leaving my lover silent and servile. I walked around him, stalking him like prey. "We're done when I say we are done. Understand?"

The coven of misfits looked at the two of us with a mixture of shock and concern. They no doubt saw Enon as the top of the magical food chain. They hadn't met anyone stronger than him. There was nothing more disappointing than watching one's mentor getting kicked in the nuts by a girl half his size.

Enon tracked my movements and tapped his lips in response to my question. I stopped in front of him. "Talk," I said to release his mutism.

He licked his lips to freshen them up and smiled at me. "Kneel."

Before I could laugh at his presumption of authority, I was on the floor in front of him. I felt the drag on my power as I had during the battle with my coven, but this time, it was being used against me.

He took delight in my slow comprehension. "Don't you see, lover? We are still bound. What's mine is yours and what's yours... is mine." The statement hit me like tons of bricks.

This was the trade-off for really great sex. Domination. Fuck.

I could feel the fire from the beast warming just under my skin. It wanted to come out and play. And oh, how I wanted to let it this time. I may have volunteered for the union when I thought it would help me rid myself of an extraneous soul, but now I was certain Enon had overstepped his boundaries. He was using me. My body. My power.

The bottles in the room were rattling as if an undetectable earthquake were happening.

"Hey, maybe we should take a break." Zeus popped into view beside us. He was sweating profusely.

I didn't break my stare, and neither did Enon.

"Enon." Zeus tried to shake his shoulder, but he was immobile. His stare wasn't the only thing made of stone at the moment. Zeus turned to me and raised his hand cautiously to my shoulder. The moment his hand hit me, I heard him whisper in the back of my mind. "Hennie," he said with a question in his voice. "Why don't we go upstairs and get a drink? Please?" he added.

I looked at him. Fresh beads of sweat were making their way down his forehead. I turned to look at the others. They were sweating too. There was even a warble of heat blurring my vision. I looked at the wine jiggling on the shelf. It wasn't an earthquake moving them. The liquid inside was boiling.

Was *I* doing this?

I didn't have to ask. I knew the answer.

"Jesus!" I dropped back on my heels and pressed my hands over my face and shook my head. The room cooled instantly. "I'm sorry. I'm sorry." I murmured to myself, to them, and to Him—if he was listening.

"It's okay." Zeus was still touching my shoulder.

I looked up at him. "It's not okay." I looked at all of them. "You don't understand what I am."

"Zeus is right." Enon stood and headed to the stairs. "We need a drink." He headed up without regard to anything he had just witnessed. Wasn't he afraid of the raw anger living inside of me? Or was he drawn to it?

Raven headed upstairs and Puck followed quickly behind her. Vlad started up the steps, stomping his feet loudly. "Vlad," I called to him. "Stay a moment?" He stopped and looked back at me suspiciously. "Alone," I added.

Zeus exchanged a look with him before retracting his hand from me. He gave me a solemn glance before heading upstairs. He seemed disappointed I had chosen Vlad to be alone with.

Vlad waited until he passed before dropping his heavy footfalls back down the stairs. I stayed in my submissive position on the floor and waited for him to stop in front of me. He wasn't afraid of me either, or at least he wanted to appear as if he wasn't.

I reached up and unbuttoned the first few buttons on my shirt. His eyes widened, and he glanced toward the stairs. When I stopped and pulled the fabric aside, he relaxed again. "Can you heal this?"

He pinched his lips together and shook his head. "If it's a magically bound affliction, I can't do much."

"Can you try?"

Vlad glanced at the stairs nervously. "He won't like me meddling with it."

"Please."

He grimaced and kneeled down before me. "Why would you want it gone?" he asked. "I would give anything to share his power." Vlad pressed his hand against my chest.

"Don't you already?" I asked.

Vlad shook his head. "He isn't fully integrated. He said it would be too much power. You're the first person I've ever seen him share his power with."

There was that phrase again—his power. Wasn't it the other way around? Enon was undoubtedly powerful, but if my shadow was correct, he wasted most of his energies maintaining his human form.

"You must be very special for him to want to recruit you."

"Yeah, I'm the bee's knees," I grumbled. "What about you? How did you get... recruited?"

Vlad lowered his hand. "Sorry, I'm not making much of a dent." He moved to get up, but I grabbed his hand. He looked down at the contact with discomfort.

"Tell me," I whispered.

"Why should I tell you anything?" he snapped, returning to his combative mode.

I looked down at his hand in mine. I massaged my finger over his palm. He watched me doing it—baffled by the contact. "When I joined the convent, I wasn't allowed to merge with the coven for several weeks. At first, I thought it was a punishment of sorts, but I think it gave me time to get to know the women. To get comfortable. That's why this merge isn't working, Vlad. We—none of us—are comfortable with each other. Becoming part of a coven requires exposure. That's why nudity helps further the process."

Vlad's eyes widened again. I caught him glance down at my cleavage. "We don't do things that way here."

"That's fine." I pushed up onto my knees, putting us closer, nearly eye to eye. He flinched, but otherwise stood his ground. "But if you want this to work, you are going to have to expose yourself in other ways."

"Expose myself?" he whispered.

"Yes," I said seductively. I wasn't usually the seducing type, but I was curious why this group had become a team to begin with. Had Enon brought them together, or had they been in a coven before this?

Vlad was such a skittish sort. Any attempt at intimidation would have sent him running upstairs in a huff. Bribes wouldn't work either. I could tell his inclination toward healing made him protective of his friends. Since I wanted answers, I needed to become one of his friends. "Tell me about yourself. How did you come to be with this coven?"

Vlad looked down at my hand, touching his, as if considering the aforementioned huff before answering. "I was lost. I thought I could fix it all. Enon found me."

"Found you?" I asked.

"Yeah, he saved me."

"Saved you?"

"He... stopped the bullet." My eyes flickered over Vlad's. "I was going to kill myself, but he showed me a different path. He showed all of us a different path."

I clenched my jaw and swallowed hard. "All of you were going to...?"

"I don't think Raven ever got that far. She had... other stuff going on. Puck was gonna kill some kid. And Zeus..." Vlad looked toward the stairs again. "He was gonna kill a lot of people."

"Enon stopped all of you from hurting someone?" I asked.

"Yeah. He said we needed to put our pain to good use."

"So, now you help him hunt demons and steal."

"It's not theft—it's payment. If people knew the good we were doing, they would gladly pay us for it."

"Pay you for what, exactly?"

"For removing demons from the Earth."

"Removing?" I repeated. I bit my lip, not wanting to continue this interrogation since I knew it was going nowhere good. "So, you hunt down demons and help Enon do what, exactly?"

"Exorcise them," Vlad answered as if I were stupid for asking. "Isn't that how you met? Weren't you possessed?"

"It's kind of a blur still," I answered with mild amusement. "What happens to the demons once they're removed?"

Vlad frowned at me—once again, I was the ignorant one in this conversation. "He sends them back to hell where they belong."

"Of course," I whispered. "Because all demons belong in hell, right?"

"Yeah," Vlad agreed.

"Vlad." I moved my hand to his shoulder. He shifted to look at the contact but allowed it. "Where does Enon get his power from?"

Vlad narrowed his eyes at me. "Where do you think he gets his power from? Just because he's a fallen doesn't mean he can't still help people."

I sucked in a breath, trying to hide my shock. "Enon is a fallen *angel*?" I said the word carefully, as if the designation might burst the room into flames.

"Of course. Why else would he hunt demons and save us from ourselves? He's doing God's work."

I groaned out my next exhale, trying not to burst into tearful laughter. "That's wonderful," I managed to get out.

"Do you know why he shared his power with you?" Vlad asked. I sensed this was an area of confusion for the entire group. Despite Enon bringing this team together, he hadn't even fully merged with the coven. For him to show up one night with a new girl he had temporarily bonded himself to must have been a kick in the face to his long-time devotees.

In all fairness, he had probably bonded to many other women. They just died before they could meet the group.

"Initially, it was to assist the exorcism," I said. "I was a weak soul. I don't think he expected me to survive." I smiled, finding some private amusement in Enon's underestimation of me.

"Well, you are very lucky." Vlad glanced down at the brand on my chest. "Any of us would jump at the chance of being connected to him. To feel his grace." He drew away from my contact. His expression told me he was on the verge of a tantrum.

"It will fade," I reminded him.

He nodded and stood up. He headed back to the stairs, but turned back with a thought. "If you really want to get rid of the connection, you should surrender to the coven. Our new bonds will automatically burn off all old spells, including contractual ones." He headed upstairs while I considered my options.

Chapter 22

AFTER A MOMENT TO collect myself, I headed up to the main floor where the tavern was. The long room was brightly lit and adorned with as much Irish paraphernalia as one space could hold. I saw my misfit crew sitting at a table under a Hennigan's light. Vlad looked over at me, then they all looked over. Nearly simultaneously, they all looked down again, trying to hide the fact that they were talking about me.

It was nothing new to me. I wasn't a big fan of my high school days. Even so, it was difficult to be the outsider even among outsiders. It was moments like this that I hated being human. I hated that I wanted to be accepted and loved. There was no spell for that. Not really. Not without enslaving someone. The heart had free will, too.

Rather than interrupt their gossip time, I headed to the bar. Enon noted my disassociation but didn't wave me over. I thought he might join me, but Raven put her arm across his shoulders and whispered in his ear. He laughed at whatever she said, which made her grin with satisfaction. She broadcasted that grin for me to see before sinking back into her chair to gloat. I snorted out loud and slid onto a barstool.

It was all starting to make sense. The doe eyes and paternal worship. If this crew had been devil worshipers, then perhaps he could have admitted he was a demon. Instead, he presented himself as a savior. An *angel*, for fuck's sake. He was claiming to be a Sister Aggie—exorcising demons under the umbrella of godly deeds.

And I'd thought *my* presence here had been sacrilegious

Poor Raven thought she was in love with a fallen angel. She was in the middle of a love story with Nicolas Cage when, in reality, she was getting into bed with Al Pacino. No wonder she fawned all over him. She wasn't about to let an angel slip through her fingers.

Neither would I, I suppose. But angels didn't come knocking on my door. All I got was demon hunters, murderers, and the devil in various forms.

I thought about Dane for a moment—as much as my heart could stand. He had at least loved me. When everyone had abandoned me, he'd stayed by me. There was room to argue he had been hunting me the entire time, but I refused to believe that. I needed to believe it was the beast inciting his predatory instincts, not me. I was just trapped in the middle. Unfortunately, being trapped between a hunter and his prey still left me in a lethal situation.

"What can I get you?" the bartender asked, snapping me out of my self-pity.

"Oh, I'm sorry, I don't have any money with me," I said, once again remembering I had left my purse in a semi-trailer in the middle of the desert. I felt bad for whoever discovered that mess of cooked beef.

"Don't need money," the bartender said. "You're a guest of the owner." He nodded his head to Enon. He lifted his glass of beer to me. I should have guessed he owned the place. Hell, after a thousand years, he probably owned half the country.

As a tribute to the bar, I ordered an Irish whiskey. A moment later it arrived warm and with far less in the glass than I would have preferred.

"Poor Hennie." My shadow sat down beside me on a stool. With the long mirror behind the bar, it was easy to see him. With the entire room visible, our conversation was unavoidable. I could almost see the beast too, but it was only a flicker in my peripheral vision. The moment I tried to focus on its reflection, it was gone again. I imagined it was a lot like trying to see the back of one's head. Without an extra mirror, it wouldn't happen. "Just when you think things are looking up—"

"You show up," I retorted quietly, so the bartender didn't think I was insane. Although, since his boss associated with an odd group anyway, I was certain he would ignore me if he heard me. "Why don't you be useful and tell me how to break my connection to Enon?"

"You can't. The magic is binding. You will have to wait until the wound heals naturally."

"That could be weeks."

"A few more days and the link will weaken. That's why he wants you to merge with the coven so badly. It would be a more permanent connection for him to access. He'll do anything to get his fix. And I do mean anything." I glanced at Enon. He was keeping me in the corner of his eye. Not quite watching me, but monitoring my location. My shadow was right. The minute I headed for the door, he would follow me. Lure me back with sexy showers.

"Can he be killed?" I asked, even though I didn't think we had reached that stage of desperation yet.

"Not in a traditional sense. His body isn't real, so you can't damage it. You would have to exorcise him from the earth, much like pulling a demon from a body."

I sighed. "Why do I get the feeling that prying him off this realm would be like trying to pick up a glued penny with slippery fingers?"

My shadow nodded. "Because you are a very intuitive woman."

"What should I do?"

My shadow's eyes widened, and he tipped his head. "You're asking me for advice?"

"Why not? You're all I have left. My last boyfriend tried to kill me. My new boyfriend is stripping me of power. At this point, I can't imagine you could steer me any further into the ditch than any of them."

"How flattering," he said snidely. "Your power will always be your power. Regardless of how the risen presents himself, you are still stronger than him. However..." My shadow glanced behind me, looking at what I couldn't see. "You must control your temper."

"A lesson I've struggled with all my life."

"Truer words were never spoken." My shadow stood and leaned into me. "If you don't learn to control it, then you will cause an apocalypse."

"What a load of horseshit," Enon said as he arrived behind him. He was staring into the mirror behind the bar, but not at me. He was looking at my shadow.

CHAPTER 23

I WASN'T SURE WHO looked more surprised, me or my shadow. He even glanced at me before returning his gaze to Enon. In the meantime, Enon set his beer down next to me and took the seat my shadow had recently vacated. "Half-truths are what the devil likes to tell. Apparently, he'll even tell them to himself when necessary."

I looked at my shadow, but there wasn't an ounce of deception in anything he had told me. "He isn't lying. I know when someone is lying," I said, sounding more defensive of my shadow than I had intended.

"You know when a lie has been spoken. You don't know if someone is hiding necessary details from you."

"And what am I hiding?" my shadow asked.

"You keep telling her an apocalypse will come if she maintains herself in this form."

"That is true."

"Yes, but you aren't telling her what that means. Why don't you give her the entire history lesson, instead of just the current events?"

My shadow didn't offer any further explanation. Judging by the look on his face, the only thing his mouth would have to contribute to this conversation was venom.

"Enon said humans had been through a dozen apocalypses already. What does that mean?" I pointedly asked him, demanding the whole truth. My shadow hissed with disapproval, and his reflection disappeared between my blinks. I frowned, insulted he would opt to abandon me rather than face a lie detector. "Asshole," I grumbled and took a sip of my liquor.

Enon laughed at my expense. "You really have quite the complex, don't you? Split personality doesn't begin to cover it." He settled in to drink his beer.

"What did you mean by that?" I asked when it was clear he wouldn't be a fountain of free-flowing information, either.

"By what?" he asked, as if the earlier conversation had already slipped his mind. I noticed he was looking at a small television next to the register. Nice to know an impending apocalypse wasn't as important as a soccer game.

"Hey!" I kicked his foot, and he finally looked at me. "What?"

"You said we could talk about the apocalypse later. It is now later, so talk."

He sighed and shifted to face me. "Do you even know what an apocalypse is?"

"The end of the world."

"No, well, yes, potentially, but that can't happen. The end of the world would be exactly what it implies, an end of life—all life. Dinosaur-level extinction. There has only ever been one terminus human apocalypse and as far as I understand it was a complete disaster. So, that doesn't happen anymore."

"If it doesn't happen anymore, then how has there been multiple apocalypses?"

"They were apocalyptic events, but they all got nipped in the bud. They would have ultimately led to the end of the world, but an intervention prevented it from reaching that stage."

"You mean God intervened."

"Yes."

"Doesn't that go against the rules?"

Enon shrugged. "Humans have the perception that free will is all-encompassing. And for the most part, that's true. Idiots get themselves killed all the time using their free will. They get other people killed too. The problem is when too many people get killed. When a set of events creates a chain reaction that will ultimately cause the demise of the human race—that is called an apocalypse."

"And that's happened before."

"Of course, humans are stupid." I rolled my eyes, offended on behalf of my borrowed species. "But where stupidity begins, that's where free will ends. If a few countries want to go to war, that's fine. But if a scientist invents a plague that will cause a holocaust—which will ultimately lead to extinction—then God steps in."

"How? What does he do?"

"He stops the game." Enon pointed to the television where the screen had paused. "He rewinds." He rolled his finger and the images on the screen reversed. "And He starts it over in a spot before things went wrong." The game played as normal on the television, minus the last few scored points. "Haven't you ever experienced déjà vu?" Enon asked.

"Lots of times."

"Well, then, that's one of his reset points. Everybody has them. Seemingly insignificant moments in their lives, but they are actually pivotal points that contribute to an apocalyptic event."

"The butterfly effect?" I asked.

"Precisely. Every reset requires integral things to be changed in order to avoid the same end result. Something as trivial as the outfit you choose to wear could ultimately cause a domino effect that spurs an apocalyptic event. Days, weeks, or even years down the line."

"What happens after the reset?"

"Nothing. Humans go back to normal. They have no idea millions of tiny details have been changed—like the lines of computer code. A little residual déjà vu here and there—aka glitches—but otherwise business as usual. Apocalypse averted... again."

"I'm assuming you know about this because you don't get reset."

"Nope, I had to relive 1945 three times before he got it right."

"Is that because you aren't technically human?"

"Yes."

"That's kind of sad."

"What, that I'm not human?"

"No, that humans keep almost killing themselves."

"Life's a stage, remember. If the director didn't jump in once in a while, the play would suck." Enon took the last drink of his beer and called to the bartender for another one. After he had a fresh glass, he swiveled back to face me. "You mind telling me what that was about downstairs? That little display?"

I paused a moment to consider my answer. Enon wasn't the type of guy I wanted as an enemy, but I wouldn't pretend he wasn't pissing me off. "I don't like my power being used against me."

"Just so we're clear, you used your power against me first. I was just defending myself."

"You weren't in danger. The only ones in danger were your coven. I used my power because you had absolutely no sympathy for their pain."

"My coven can handle it."

"Says who? I know what you told them, Enon. You may have saved them from suicidal and homicidal tendencies, but you have no right to claim the title of an angel."

"I never told them I was—"

"You never told them you were a risen either."

"And how is that conversation supposed to go? You'd never even heard of a risen. At least they understand what an angel is—or at least what the dictionary definition of one is."

"They think you are doing God's work," I hissed.

"I am. I'm still ridding the world of demons, aren't I?"

"Oh, you arrogant prick."

"Why am I arrogant? Because I don't exorcise demons with a rosary in my hand?"

"No, you do it with a knife in your hand. Your victims don't even survive."

Enon raised his finger at me. "Those were mercy kills. I've never killed for pleasure."

"Says the man who eats demons."

"Oh, please!" he said through clenched teeth. "You are such a hypocrite."

"Hypocrite?"

"Yes, you're the freaking devil, Hennie. And *you're* judging *me* about things you couldn't possibly understand."

"I understand the truth, and I refuse to be a part of this coven when you are lying to them about your identity."

"What's the lie? I'm not claiming to be human."

"They need to know you're a demon."

"I am as much a demon as you are the devil."

"Fine, then explain that you're a risen, but they can't continue to believe you are an angel."

"What does it matter? You don't know what an angel is any more than those four."

"I know the difference between good and evil."

Enon scoffed and sputtered out a bout of laughter before he could speak. "Good!" He took a breath and exhaled it as he leaned toward me. "If an angel *fell*—" He air-quoted *fell*. "—onto Main Street, I guarantee anyone who didn't piss themselves outright would be praying to God for mercy. Trust me, Hennie, they are much better off with a runaway demon in their midst than the sentinels of the fucking universe, so stop talking about things you don't understand." Enon turned away, panting from the exertion of his argument. His hands were shaking, and he could barely lift his beer without spilling it into his lap.

Once he had control of his choler, he spoke again. "I get it." He looked over the mirror ahead of us, as if searching for my shadow. "You're afraid I'm going to trap you." He reached up and dipped his fingers into his shirt, touching his brand. "Afraid that once I have you, I won't let you go." He raised his other hand to my chest and touched my brand through the fabric. "My only question is. What's so bad about that? You haven't exactly minded my company so far, have you?"

I licked my lips and shook my head. "It's not your company, I mind, Enon. It's about handing you a ticking time bomb."

"Ah." Realization seemed to hit him and he retracted his contact. He scooted his stool closer to mine and sat back down. He put his feet under my stool, tangling our legs together. "You think I'm power-hungry." He rested his hand over mine on the bar.

"Aren't you?"

"You know, you don't quite make sense—what you are. You're like a little ball of fire that doesn't burn." He rubbed his thumb over my skin. "It's sweet, but your altruistic nature makes you see the world as black and white. The reality of me is I couldn't care less about power beyond my own needs. I behave just like a human, and I have for the last millennium. I eat as much as I want, I sleep as often as I need to, and I fuck as hard and as long as my partners can stand." His other hand was on my leg now, sliding up the fabric of my jeans.

I glanced at the contact. "Then I suppose it's about control. You want my power, therefore you need to control me."

"No, this is about a mutually beneficial arrangement," Enon said flatly, and pulled both his hands away. "You... How shall I put this delicately? You are an idiot."

I scoffed. "Excuse me?"

"Oh, sorry, let me qualify that. You are a very powerful idiot."

"It's starting to feel a little warm in here, Enon," I warned.

He smirked and leaned on the bar. "Look, you are amazing and I'd be lying if I didn't say I wanted to fuck you silly until the end of this century, but the reality is you are going to need a lot of work."

"Work?"

"You see, you don't actually know how to use your power."

"I think I've proven—"

"You've proven that you can create pain when you get pissed off. Let's face the facts here, Hennie. If it weren't for this link between us, you would not have gotten away from your coven. I did all that with *your* power." He leaned in a little closer. "Because I'm not an infant."

"I'm not an—"

"With respect to your lifespan and knowledge, you are. Don't get me wrong, if you had the memories that belong to this soul, I would be kneeling before you long before you ever demanded it. And yeah, I'm not the good guy." Enon glanced back at his crew. "Not like they think I am, anyway." He stood up and pulled out his wallet. Despite being the owner of the establishment, or perhaps because he was, he took a pinch of hundreds from the leather fold and tossed it on the bar. Aside from my curiosity about the interest-bearing potential for a thousand-year-old IRA, I wondered if the bartender received hush money for the odd happenings and conversations going on in the building.

"If I were a good guy, I would take the time to help you control and hone your skills, so you weren't a complete magical spaz. However, not only do we not have time for that, I don't have much patience. So instead..." Enon dragged his finger down my arm. "I'm going to use all my guile and charm to get you to merge with the coven. Then I'll drink you in—as much as I can stand. When I've had my fill, then I'll burn all that energy, pleasuring you in any way I can." Enon reached around, pulling me forward with a firm grip on my ass. "But more importantly, with my self-interest at the heart of your survival, I will do anything to protect you. I will wield your power for you and kill anyone—"

"Not kill," I corrected, suddenly removed from all my carnal thoughts.

Enon slipped out of his seduction mode and released my ass. "Yeah, sure, Hennie. Because that's how we'll get you out of this situation. Everybody lives. No one dies. And you get to live happily ever after." He chuckled to himself and walked away.

I noted the glare I was receiving across the bar from Raven. She had no doubt watched every second of our intense interaction. I ignored her and took down the last of my whiskey. I didn't bother to look up at the mirror before I spoke.

"Is he right? I'm not skilled enough to protect myself."

"He would offer a tactical advantage," my shadow answered. "One that could prevent you from accidentally starting an apocalypse. It's a dangerous option, though. There are no guarantees his desires will remain focused purely on human satisfactions. If you do succeed in staving off the coven, you may still have to deal with him later."

"Maybe by that time I'll be skilled enough to get rid of him."

"Maybe. Maybe not."

I huffed out a breath. "Regardless, right now, it seems to be my only option."

Chapter 24

"*H*ennie," my name whispered across the bar. I looked at the misfit coven, trying to determine who was calling me, but they were deep in conversation and laughing at the lewd gestures Vlad was making.

"*Hennie.*" It whispered again, and this time I knew it was Dane's voice.

I looked left and right, searching the bar for his face, but he wasn't here. Neither was his voice, I supposed. The whispers were only in my mind. As if there weren't enough voices in my head already.

"*Hennie.*"

I slipped off the barstool and followed Dane's voice like the call of a siren. I stepped outside the bar and saw him in the middle of the street. The sun was down, and at some point, it had started misting. The minuscule raindrops looked more like fog than actual rain.

Dane was standing there, completely dry despite the damp weather. He was staring back at me. It was that first moment in the hotel room all over again. Relief, anguish, and something more.

Something I was still reluctant to call love. I wasn't sure I was capable of that anymore. Though my shadow seemed to insist he was full of love, I didn't feel that. I felt empty.

Even the addition of the beast into my repertoire hadn't changed that; it just spurred on my already short-fused temper.

As reality seeped back in, I whipped my head around, searching for the rest of the coven. Surely this was a trap. Dane Pratchett was the very best bait.

"They aren't here," he said. "Technically, neither am I."

"No?" I asked. "Then where are you?"

"Home. Things have changed since we last saw you."

"Well, attempted murder does do that to people."

"She believes you now."

I pinched my lips and stepped off the curb. I was well aware I was walking toward the man that was hunting me, walking toward the bait, but I needed to get a clearer view of his face.

Clearer indeed. The moment I stepped into the first car lane, the city-scape disappeared, replaced by my own living room. I could still feel the misting rain and the chill in the air, but all my eyes could see were the plush furnishings of my parents' former home. Hennie's parents.

However, much like Dane wasn't really here in the rain with me, I was not there in my living room with him. He reached forward, leaning on the back of the couch. If he was feeling what I was, he probably wanted to leap over it and hug me. Hopefully, hug me.

His eyes danced over me. His lips held the same unspoken sentiments. Oh, how I wished my story was one of romance. I wanted so much to be the damsel, but I wasn't. I was the damned.

"What does who believe?" I asked when the silence between us became tormenting.

"Rachel. She now believes God gave you permission to be here."

I scoffed. "You mean now that I'm the walking evidence of it, she believes me? Way to get on board, Rach."

"She wanted you to know," Dane whispered.

"Okay, well, thanks. You can relay this to her: eat shit and—"

"Hennie, we don't have much time." My enthusiasm for my insult died away. It was as if Dane had told me he didn't have long to live. "I'm doing this on my own. It's taking a lot to hold the between open."

I blinked at the magical reference. Dane was picking up the craft quickly. I wondered if I could have gained my skills faster without the overload of drug-induced lulls. Or perhaps Rachel was just a good teacher.

Enon was right. I had fallen behind in my studies. The occasional smack talk did not a witch make.

"Magic looks good on you," I admitted. I presumed the looking good part also had to do with his sloppy hair and chin stubble. As I looked over his face, I noticed he looked thinner. I couldn't tell from his clothes, but either he had lost some muscle tone, or he had lost his winter layers. I yearned to reach out and pull back his shirt collar to reveal the ink stitched onto his chest.

"I haven't been sleeping," Dane said, as if defending his appearance. "I haven't been eating." I looked up into his eyes and noticed the darkness beneath them. I also noticed the moisture gathering along his lower lids. "I've missed you," he whispered, making my heart ache with the honesty of it.

I opened my mouth, trying to form the words I wanted, but hated, to admit. "I missed you too."

Dane's face pinched, and he shook his head. He clenched his jaw, fighting the emotions that were overwhelming him. "Who is he?" he seethed.

I looked away, ashamed of the pain I was putting on his face. I could remind Dane he was my enemy now. I could remind him that sharing my bed was no longer an option for him, but of course, he knew that. He wasn't asking out of rational jealousy. He was asking because heartbreak was all we could share now.

"Who is he?" he asked again, showing more anger. His hands were no longer braced on the back of the couch, but embedded. His nails were even puncturing the fabric.

"His name is Enon. He's a risen." Dane's eyes narrowed with an unspoken question. "He's a demon that has escaped hell and taken on an artificial human form."

Dane's eyes blanked the moment I said the word *demon*. Had he been able to grab me and shake me at that moment, he would have. "You're fucking a demon?"

I blinked, disliking the succinct version of my relationship status. "It's a circumstantial relationship," I answered lamely. "I'm bound to him." I tugged on my shirt to reveal the insignia to him again. His eyes locked on it with disdain.

"Why did you bind yourself to him?"

"The binding was part of the exorcism process. Hennie and I had to be separated. He just grabbed onto the wrong piece. But before you ask, Hennie is fine. She's... well, I assume in heaven. At any rate, she's not—"

"Is it temporary?"

"Yes, once it heals, I'll have full control again."

Dane's head tipped back slightly, as if he were listening to something. Then his eyes lit with a new level of offense. "You're sharing your power with him."

"Not voluntarily, but yes."

"You need to leave him, Hennie," Dane said urgently. "He's dangerous."

"As opposed to the safe bosom of my former coven, who is trying to throw me back into hell? Or should I return to you—the man who has been hunting me from the very beginning?"

Dane's face shrank, though he didn't shift his gaze into the telltale shame I thought he would. "I know it doesn't make sense. The way I feel about you is... confusing. I never lied about my desire to hunt you. But the moment you walked out of that hospital room, you were no longer the woman I knew. You were something feral, like me. I knew the hunt was over. It was time to kill."

I took in a breath, trying not to let those words cut me to the very core. Dane's hands gripped the back of the couch as if he were still fighting that urge. Perhaps he was.

His chest rose with a deep breath as a tear finally fell from his eye. "The part I find most confusing, though." Dane's brow dipped deep, and he shook his head. "The part that fills me with dread." He clenched his jaw. "Is that it was your power that made me like this. You put this hunger for evil inside of me, Hennie."

The cold around me seemed to shift, as if the very fingers of Jack Frost were trying to tickle me. I took an unintentional step back, trying to distance myself from the truth. I recalled the time during Sister Aggie's possession. The coven had still been strong, but they had been relying on my power instead of hers. The power of hell.

Even if Aggie orchestrated the plan, I carried out the deed with the coven's guidance. I'd created Dane. I'd made him a hunter.

Had he really been designed to hunt demons to protect the coven, or was that merely his cover? A wolf in sheep's clothing? How far did it go? Was his attraction to me all part of his design—to get close to me? Ready and waiting to execute me, should the need arise. Was he the failsafe in case things went wrong?

Well, things *had* gone wrong.

Very wrong.

I was beginning to understand why there was so much turmoil on Dane's face. He was a weapon against his will. He wanted to love me, but something was overriding that love. It was the dark part of him. The part that remained despite his cleansing. Dane had to be just a little broken in order to see the darkness in others. It was that part of him that wanted to kill me.

Dane glanced back as if he were listening again. I narrowed my eyes. "I thought you said you were alone," I asked, trying to figure out when the lie had gotten past me.

Dane shook his head. "I'm doing the magic on my own."

"Are they all with you?" I asked.

"No, it's only Rachel."

"Show her to me. I want to see her traitorous face."

Dane looked back and a moment later, Rachel stepped up beside him, appearing out of thin air. She glanced down at Dane's grip on the couch and rested her hand over his. His grip relaxed, as did the rest of him. After a long exhale, he rested his forehead on her shoulder. It was an almost cat-like bid for attention.

It wasn't the first time I had seen this behavior, but it was the first time it infuriated me. I hated that Rachel inspired calmness in Dane—whereas I inspired homicide. I also hated that Dane—the man she supposedly didn't trust—was now privy to the motherly goodness Rachel offered. Motherly goodness, my ass. Where had that been when *I'd* needed it? All I'd ever got from Rachel was resentment and condescension.

Rachel seemed to recognize the ire on my face and whispered something to Dane. He stood up straight and stepped back. He didn't disappear, but his image blurred just enough to make it difficult to focus on.

Rachel pulled back her veil and wimple, revealing her chaotic red hair. I wasn't sure why she did it, except perhaps to remind me that I was speaking to a fellow human and not a representative of God. Which, by now, meant very little to me. The Big Guy was far too enigmatic to be reliable. "You should be proud of Dane," she said softly. "He's been working very hard to resist his desires. The coven has been helping him."

I should have appreciated the kindness she bestowed on my lover, but I was envious of him. His violent and murderous desires provided him with an invitation into Rachel's good graces, whereas I had been thrown to the dogs. If it weren't for her, my reparations for wicked deeds would consist of dental crowns and a bad nose job. Now I had multiple lawsuits for emotional distress to pay for.

"That's very generous of you," I said coldly. "Very seraphic of you."

"I know you're mad, Hennie."

"No shit," I countered.

"I also know that I was wrong," Rachel said, as if she were about to part the seas of my anger with the admission.

I rolled my jaw a moment, trying to find the right words to express myself. "Fuck you." It wasn't the witty riposte I'd been searching for, but it was honest.

"Oh, Hennie, how did we end up here?" She rested her hip on the back of the couch.

"You stopped trusting me."

"I know, but can you blame me? I mean, really. Paula in our midst for years, then you? Do you really blame me for rejecting any potential for evil?"

I took a long breath, searching for what little empathy I had left for others. "No," I finally admitted. "I know you were protecting the coven. I just wish you would have protected me, too."

Rachel frowned. "You're right."

I rolled my eyes at her prescribed negotiation dialogue.

"No, I'm serious. I can see my mistakes plain as day now. You were a ticking time bomb, but better to have you with us than be vulnerable to the devil's influence. I understand why Sister Aggie brought you to us."

"Yeah, but that backfired, too. Just like Paula's plot to trap me into my promise backfired. Just like everything everyone has ever done to *help* me has backfired."

"We've all made mistakes, Hennie—especially me."

"Why is that? Why so many mistakes?" I asked. "Doesn't He talk to you?" I motioned to the proverbial heavens. "What does He say you should do with me?"

Rachel's brow twitched downward before she answered. "He wants me to help you." I didn't need any special gift to detect this lie. The slightly too cheerful smile on her face said it all.

"Don't lie to me, Rachel," I said flatly. "It's as much an insult to my intelligence as it is to yours."

Rachel sighed and rubbed her face. "Fine, you want the truth? He doesn't tell me crap about you." Her voice no longer held the motherly tone of a Sister Superior. She was just Rachel again. "I have been praying since day one for a sign, but He has never given me one. He's never actually told me to remove you."

"So, why are you still pursuing me?"

"Because!" Rachel laughed, but it wasn't out of humor so much as frustration. "Oh, Hennie, you don't see it, do you?" There were tears in her eyes now. "You don't see how powerful you are. How dangerous you are?"

"In case you haven't been paying attention, I haven't been using my power. I've been living happily as a normal human being—give or take a few incidents. I'm not the black-eyed sadist Paula wanted me to be. This power is neutral. I won't hurt anyone, I promise."

Rachel's eyes flickered over me. "Let me show you." She moved around the couch and I took a step back, effectively stepping into the coffee table. She stopped in front of me and extended her hands. I was wary of this seemingly friendly offer. "I'm going to shift the view. I need a little contact so I can show you what I see when I look at you. I won't hurt you," she added.

It wasn't a lie, but for some reason, I looked back at Dane. As if he would protect me.

I raised my hands over Rachel's and pressed them down. It didn't feel like skin-to-skin contact. It felt like two magnets repelling each other. I couldn't quite touch her, but the pressure between us felt a little like contact.

A trickle of her power came through the connection and I felt the desire to curl up in her arms, much like I imagined Dane felt being near her. She was a warm blanket on a wintry day. So much so that my muscles relaxed. My head lolled and my eyes closed as I wallowed in her adopted divinity.

For a moment, I wondered what my magic felt like to her. Was it carnal like the grip of hell? Was it neutral, like the Earth? Or was it the same invigorating icy heat I felt?

When I opened my eyes again, we were back in the street. Dane was still in the background, blurred by the rain. Rachel was smiling at me warmly. "How's that?" she asked, as if the transition might have hurt me. Maybe she'd thought it would. Did she think her power would be repulsive to me? Was I supposed to shrink from the sunlight and cower from garlic as well?

"Always a pleasure." I meant to say it mockingly, but it was too true to pull that off.

"Look around," she instructed.

I did as she said and looked around. I didn't understand what I was supposed to see. The city was quiet. The street was empty. It was dark except for the streetlight down the block.

"Look again." She closed her eyes, exerting some kind of power on the view.

When I looked again, I saw glowing cracks in the street. Some even traveled up the sides of the buildings and through the glass of the windows like an overlapping image. The incandescent glow was subtle, but enough to know there was something on the other side of these rifts.

In another scenario, I might have asked the necessary questions. What is this? What's happening? Why is it like this? But I already knew what she was showing me. I was fragmenting reality, much as I had fragmented myself.

This earthly dimension was being ripped apart by an aberrant presence.

And that aberration was me.

I was breaking the whole damn world.

"This is why I am still searching for you. This is why I can't stop. It doesn't matter that you *can* be here, Hennie. It only matters that you *shouldn't* be here."

"I can stop using my power if you stop hunting," I rationalized.

"It doesn't matter if you use the power. You *are* the power. You affect everything around you, whether you mean to or not." Rachel frowned at me. "I know you don't want to hurt anyone. I was stupid and selfish not to recognize that sooner. I know you will do the right thing. Which is why I need you to surrender."

I glared at her, infuriated by her guilt-laden attack. "I can't surrender to my own death," I said.

"I know," Rachel said somberly. "I don't like it any more than you do. I wish there was another way, but I can't protect you for the sake of the entire world." Rachel bypassed the repellent magnetism and pressed her palms into mine. "It's time for you to come home," she said firmly.

The vision of my living room returned, though a little different from before. I looked down at the coffee table to my left. Dane was still behind the couch—clearer than before. I felt Rachel's soft hands clasping onto mine. I also felt warm, dry air delivered by indoor heat.

This was no longer a vision. Rachel had just brought me home.

Chapter 25

My mouth draped in shock as I scanned my new surroundings. Eventually, my outrage at the abduction triggered a response. "You bitch!"

I raised a fist to punch her, but Dane was behind me in a flash, lassoing my body. I was up and colliding with the floor before I realized I was no longer on my own two feet. I didn't wait to see if he could resist his murderous instincts this time around.

"Off!" I yelled and Dane flew back—though not nearly as far as he should have.

I got to my feet just as Rachel reached me. I barreled into her, pushing her onto the couch linebacker-style. Once I was on top of her, I balled my fist and drew back for a hard swing. I should have been using my power. After all, what was the point of being an uber witch if you couldn't whoop some ass? But my power was the last thing on my mind at that moment. This was personal, and I wanted to keep it that way. I wanted to feel her jaw crack under the weight of my human fist.

And crack it did.

Rachel's chin shifted to the side, unnaturally. The breaking sound coincided with her yelp of pain. It was what I had wanted—or at least what I'd thought I had wanted—but there was only one problem.

My fist never touched her.

My arm was retracted, and my knuckles were primed for impact when the injury happened.

The mere thought of hurting her had created the event.

Shocked and guilt-ridden, I froze and stared at her. She looked back at me, frightened—the concern I usually saw on her face was gone. It was all fear now.

Dane tackled me and we rolled off the couch to the floor. I kicked and clawed at him, but I was afraid of defending myself too much now. I wanted to hurt them, but not debilitate them.

Dane got behind me and clamped my arms down. Rachel came into view. A quick swipe of her hand and her jaw was back together again. I looked around, searching for the rest of the team, but they really weren't around. Paula wasn't even here to gloat.

Why?

Why attack me with only two, when the entire team hadn't been enough before?

Rachel kneeled down before me and pressed her hand to my chest. I felt her feel-good vibe stifle what little fight I had left in me.

I struggled against Dane's grip, searching for the anger to withstand her quelling control. Where was the beast? Where was the bitterness that inspired my deepest power to rise? Everything was gone. I didn't have the will to hurt them the way I needed to. Enon was right: my survival depended on "kill or be killed," but I didn't *want* to kill them.

This was why they were working alone. They knew I cared for them. They knew it would be harder for me to hurt them, especially close up.

"It's okay, Hennie," Rachel whispered. "It's not going to hurt."

"Don't," I whispered back. "He let me stay," I pleaded with the only defense I had, the only sliver of hope I had ever had for my existence. I wasn't the devil. I was good. I was human. I was important.

Wasn't I?

Rachel frowned and poured her magic into me. The opposite spectrum of power was just as addictive, but far less jarring to one's body. I could feel her grabbing onto me as if she were reaching in to pull out my heart. Except it wasn't my heart she was tugging on, it was my soul. She was going to pull me right out of my body. A fast and dirty exorcism.

The irony, of course, was that she never would have used this kind of force on me if Hennie was still around. She never would have endangered the physical body if there was still a soul to save. But with the original soul out of the way, Rachel could rip this body apart if necessary.

I was feeling less guilty about the jaw-breaking now.

"Dane," I whimpered, hoping he might help me. Defend me against this death sentence.

Dane leaned down and pressed a kiss to my cheek. I could feel the tears on his cheek. "I love you," he whispered. It would have been sweet if he hadn't been assisting in my death.

Rachel's ethereal grip tightened on my soul—ready to displace it with one yank. She looked at Dane and nodded. He shifted his arm under my chin, locking the crook of his elbow against my throat. This was the ultimate play then. Displace my soul and kill the body.

Oh, that was good.

And Rachel was right. There would be no pain. Dane wasn't officially killing anyone, just disposing of my human wrapper, so I couldn't return to it. It would also prevent any other foreign invaders from housing in it.

Clever.

Rachel took in a deep breath and held it while she looked at me. She looked like she wanted to say some final goodbye.

What was left to say?

Have a nice trip back to hell? Farewell and good riddance? It's not you, it's me?

There were no gracious speeches for killing someone and damning them to an eternity in hell. Even the tears that were welling in her eyes didn't make up for what she was doing to me. It wasn't enough of an apology for me not to hold it against her. In that moment, I knew I would add this last betrayal to the list of grievances being stored in the molten heart of the beast. She may have been saving the world from my angelic rage, but hell would suffer for it—burning that much hotter. Adding more pain to the souls already enduring a lifelong sentence of suffering.

Including my own.

Rachel looked at Dane one last time. Then, with a flourish of her hand, she pulled on the tenuous threads holding my blacklisted soul.

CHAPTER 26

*C*LUNK.

Okay, that's not actually the sound my soul made when it hit the brick wall of my brand, but it felt like it. As if my heart was letting out a single loud drum beat every time Rachel failed to pry my soul from this body.

Thump.
Thump.
Thump.

The look on her face was quite possibly the best part of the entire scene—as if she was two inches from salvation, but a piece of chewing gum was keeping her from getting any farther.

Enon lazily applauded in the background. I wasn't sure when he had arrived, but I sensed him long before Rachel shifted to reveal him. He was sitting in my armchair, relaxed and unfettered by the murder attempt before him. I could only assume he knew it wouldn't work. Why he had to wait until I was on the spit with an apple in my mouth to reveal that, I don't know.

"Wonderful," he said without glee. "More idiots."

Rachel stood up straight, more than a little offended by his accusation. "This has nothing to do with you."

"I beg to differ, Sister. Our powers are entangled." He motioned his finger over at me. "If you send Hennie back to hell, then I would go with her." He smiled mischievously. "Not that you would ever be successful in doing that in the first place, but I would appreciate it if you would stop trying."

"Release her then," Rachel insisted.

Enon tipped his lips down and tensed his neck. "Why, in God's name, would I do that?"

"Because she has to be removed," Rachel said.

"No, she doesn't."

"She doesn't belong on Earth."

"Neither do I, but a thousand years later I've made it work, with minimal backlash."

"I'm warning you." Rachel stepped forward, brandishing the magical equivalent of a cocked gun. Though it was only a flare in her energy, I knew Enon could tell it was the pee-your-pants kind of power.

"Mmm." Enon shook his head and got out of the chair. "Do you want to play with me again?" Enon lost all the humor in his voice and face. "Let me explain something to you, because I'm not quite sure you're really understanding who you're dealing with."

Rachel tipped her head to one side and glared at his cocky approach. He stopped in front of her and looked her over before proceeding to school her with his thousand-year-old knowledge.

"I grew my skills over the course of millennia while toiling away in the fires of hell. I used those skills to break every law of physics known to man. I created this body, and I fed it with the souls of demons. Now, I get where you are coming from. I mean, good God, I feel you from half a state away, and yes, that is some spicy magic you're conjuring, but I'm not human.

"You can step up to bat again and again, and you aren't going to hurt me. And even if you would succeed in vanquishing my soul, I will just come back again. Because there are no lines for dirt, sweetheart." Enon licked his lips. "Fighting me is like trying to fight the wind. You'll wear yourself out and only have messy hair to show for it."

I watched the standoff before me with interest. I wondered if Enon really was that much of a pain in the ass. I presumed since Rachel wasn't bitch-slapping him; she didn't have a valid argument. That was rather disappointing. Perhaps experience in this case *was* more important than power.

Finally, feeling like myself again, I flexed my magical muscles and threw Dane off. This time he went farther. He crashed into the wall behind the dining room table, drawing Rachel and Enon's attention. I stood and moved to Enon's side. I crossed my arms as I looked at Rachel.

"Well, I'd tell you not to—"

"Remember what Dane told you," Rachel interrupted my smack talk farewell. She motioned to Enon with her wide eyes. She looked legitimately afraid for me. God damn her. How dare she look at me like she was worried about me even after she tried to kill me? I was tired of this. I was tired of all of it. Maybe it *was* time to consider eliminating some of my enemies.

I wasn't sure how, but Enon and I were back on the street in front of the bar. The rain had stopped, but there was a rumble of thunder in the clouds above. No lightning, only the echo of cloud-to-cloud growls.

Enon said something about going inside and tugged on my hand. At some point, he must have given up trying to break me out of my melodramatic trance, because he disappeared. I was alone on the street, standing in the shadows between streetlights. I didn't even move when a car drove around me, honking on behalf of its driver's irritation.

When the rain started up again, it didn't feel cold as it had before.

It felt hot.

CHAPTER 27

"I SEE YOU'VE RESORTED to murder plots," Jess said from the corner of my bed—Enon's bed. I looked over and saw him slumbering away. I never really understood whether my interactions with Jess were a dream or whether she was actually a ghost, but it didn't matter. All I knew was she was my last safe haven. The only person who made sense—if only by not making any sense. "Do you think you could do it?"

"Why not? I'm the devil."

Jess snorted and jumped off my bed. "Maybe, but that's no excuse to kill people."

"Isn't it?" I pulled myself out of bed and followed Jess out onto the balcony that overlooked the city. I still had no idea where I was, but it didn't matter. I would leave in the morning, anyway. I was already repeating my mistakes by staying another night with Enon. "I'm open to other ideas, if you have any." I sat down in a padded lounge chair, realizing all too late why Jess had opted to lean against the railing instead of sitting in the other chair. The rain had left them a wet sponge. I groaned and looked at my drenched bottom. I ignored it and slumped back, allowing the moisture to soak into my back as well.

Jess smirked at me and took in a long sniff of the air. She spun on her toes to lean over the railing and look at the city. "I miss the rain. I hated when it rained, but I loved the smell after it was done."

"The wet dog smell of nature?" I teased.

"No, the smell of life."

"The smell of burgeoning fungus?"

Jess turned back around. She reminded me of a Disney princess gliding and spinning on tiny feet rather than walking and pivoting like the rest of us bipedal clouts. She shook her head at me like one might shake a finger. "You aren't going to sour my mood, Hennie James."

I chuckled at her determined optimism. She could find joy in almost anything. That must have been how she'd tolerated me over the years. Only Jess could make friends with the devil. "So Dane tried to kill me again." I dropped that little nugget like casual gossip.

"Bummer," she said with legitimate disappointment—albeit underplayed. "Some men just don't get foreplay."

I laughed. It was so not the time to be laughing, but it felt good. "Do you think I'll ever get to see you again?"

"What do you mean?"

"After I die?"

Jess's face went pale and her lips parted just enough to imply that she wanted to say something, but she didn't actually say anything.

"I mean, I assume you are on the topside. If I die, then I go back to the downside. Do you get vacation days?" I tried to put the humor back in and Jess smiled, but there were tears in her eyes. She slid down the railing and squatted on the short rim of cement that held the metal in place.

"I don't really know, but... well..."

"What?" I asked.

She shrugged. "I guess I figure if you are the devil, then you could do whatever you want. But of course, why would the devil want to see me?"

Tears sprang to my eyes, and I fought through the emotions to speak. "Because you're awesome!" I expounded. "And because you're the only friend I have."

Jess grimaced. "That's not entirely true."

"Don't. Don't even bring up her name."

"I know it doesn't seem like it, but it's hard for her."

"It's hard for *her*?" I squawked.

"It's hard for all of us, Hennie." Jess stood back up, swinging along the railing like she was dancing instead of just repositioning. "I mean, you are a very complex person, or being or whatever."

"Uh-huh." I crossed my arms, waiting for the psychology to begin.

"Technically speaking, you're like a split personality. You don't operate the same as other people do. The war within is a pretty literal interpretation for you."

"No kidding."

"When you think about everything you've been through, it starts to get a little twisted, like self-abuse." Jess looked at me, biting her lip. "Not that you are anything like them, but..." She waggled her head and grimaced.

What she was saying reminded me of what Dane had said about my power creating him. When the trinity split, there were proper divisions, but not me. I was a branch—or a root. Regardless of the metaphor, I was still a bit of all of them. My humanity may have balanced me out in the early stages, but the power was seeping out of me.

I was affecting the world around me. Just as my shadow was going against himself by protecting me now, there may have been a part of me then that was going against my survival by sabotaging myself.

Yes, very twisted.

"In a way, you're just hurting yourself." Jess said this to herself as if she, too, were going over every awful incident in my life and translating them as psycho-masochistic indulgences.

"I murdered you." The confession was out even before my mind had reached the accusation.

Jess looked up, brow crinkled in befuddlement. "What?"

"It was the beast. Therefore, it was me. I killed you." The words were like acid to my ears, but I had to say it. The beast was part of me, therefore I had killed my best friend.

"No, no, no!" Jess leaped to my side, ignoring the wet cushion as she sat down next to my legs. "That's not what happened." She leaned forward, brushing my hair aside as she shushed my hyperventilating breaths.

I tried to pull away from her tenderness. I didn't deserve her kindness or forgiveness or her rationalization of innocence by ignorance. "I killed my parents."

"No, you didn't!" Jess said firmly. "Paula may be a part of you, but her actions are still her own to be blamed for."

"The beast has no free will. It's a part of me and that makes me responsible for your death."

Jess's mouth dropped, and she looked at me with utter pity. I hated that, but I didn't expect her to jump up and agree with me. "Oh, Hennie." Jess picked up my hands, pushed them together, and kissed them. "I'm so sorry. I'm so, so sorry."

"Why are you apologizing to me? I'm the abomination."

Jess shook her head slowly and looked me over. "I didn't tell you because I thought it didn't matter. What's done is done. But you need to know the truth."

"What truth?"

"The beast didn't kill me."

I shook my head. "It's a fine line, but you were caught in that fire—"

"No, it wasn't the fire—I mean, it didn't help, but..." Jess pinched her eyes closed a moment. "Why is this so hard to say?"

"What?"

"Hennie, I killed myself."

I drew away from her, caught off guard by the statement. "No. Why would you set your house on fire?"

"That part was an accident. I suppose if we want to split hairs, OD-ing was an accident too."

"OD-ing? You weren't a drug user."

"Yeah, I was."

"I would have known if you were using."

Jess pinched back her lips and looked away. There was the slightest bit of anger in her eyes. She was trying to hide it, but it was easy to recognize since I rarely ever saw it on her. "When would you have noticed? You were dealing with your dad. I was in college. Then you went to the convent. We had barely spoken in the months before I died."

"Why?"

"I was in a bad place. I was depressed and feeling sorry for myself."

I shook my head. "I didn't know."

"Of course you didn't. Drug users don't advertise that they are miserable. Besides, you were going through your own shit."

"Fuck my shit! You were my friend!"

"I just took too much. The lighter dropped on the bed. My first thought was to call you. I didn't even call 911. I only called you." I leaned forward and hugged her. She draped against me, rubbing my back. "I'm sorry."

"Why are you still apologizing?"

"Because I left you, Hennie." Jess leaned back and cupped my face with her hands. "I didn't mean to add myself to the list of people who left you."

"You're the only one who hasn't given up on me."

Jess smiled at me and nodded. "I'll never give up on you. Even if I have to visit you in hell." We embraced again, engrossing ourselves in the moment for as long as it could last. Jess suddenly stiffened and gasped. "Oh, shit, I forgot!" She leaned back to look at me. "Don't—"

"—move!" another voice finished the sentence.

I was on my back, no longer on the patio or in bed. I looked around at the faces of the misfit coven standing around me. Vlad, Raven, Puck, and Zeus. Enon was standing at my head, looking down at me. "What are you doing?" I asked, noticing the straps around my ankles and wrists.

"Something I should have done when I first met you," Enon answered. "Exorcise your demon." He looked down at me, a small smile of exhilaration on his face. He also looked a little hungry.

CHAPTER 28

I MUST HAVE BEEN in a backroom in the wine cellar. I could still smell dusty wood, but also a hint of mildew. This must have been more of a utility room. I noted the heavy rock walls around me. No sense in wasting my vocal cords on volume.

Enon's coven held me down with their combined skills, and Enon anchored my magic, making me feel like a brick-shoed swimmer in my own pool of power.

"I'm not possessed, you asshole," I snapped. "Let me go." I pulled against my cloth restraints physically and magically, but I could see from the fresh blood on the table's bindings that they had infused them with potent spells. This wouldn't be an easy escape.

"Of course you are," Raven said to my left. "You're dripping with negative energy."

"I'm dripping with negative energy?" I looked back at Enon. "Maybe that's a sign you should stay away from me." Enon glanced down at me and winked as if this was just a fun party game he was playing with his friends.

"Why didn't you tell us she was possessed from the beginning?" Zeus asked.

I bent my neck to look at him. He was by my right foot. Unlike Raven, he seemed a little worried about this exorcism. I didn't look like the sick young men and women who usually had two fangs of a demon in them.

"I told you, this is a very powerful demon," Enon explained. "I didn't have the strength to remove it without you. That's why I bound myself to her." He glanced at Raven as if this explanation would make up for him cheating on her. "It was the only way to protect the vessel. She should be strong enough to extract the possessor now."

"The possessor?" My eyes widened, and a pulled against my ties again. "You aren't talking about..." I could see Enon's lip curve up. "You can't!"

"I don't know that I could normally," he admitted. "But think about what I did the first time around with our connection."

He was talking in code, trying to avoid outright saying what happened between us that first night. I thought back to the exorcism that freed Hennie. Enon had extracted a real, live human soul, untainted by hell, from this body. He wanted to replicate that experiment, only this time he wanted to take the beast.

My mind frantically tried to think if this was even possible. It wasn't a soul, but it had a lot of power. In effect, he could feed off it, but was it too much? Surely his appetite wouldn't allow for such a feast.

"This isn't an exorcism," I said as the answer came to me. Enon glanced down at me but didn't respond. "This is an invitation!" I looked around at the others. "Listen to me! He isn't the man he pretends to be. He's the only demon in this room."

Vlad, down by my left leg, chuckled and shook his head. "That's new. At least it's original. Demons will say anything to get what they want."

I turned my gaze to him and bore my eyes into his. "He eats demons. That's why you are here. You help him feed!" Vlad looked stonewalled at first, but I could see a flicker of doubt in his eyes as he thought—maybe back to a moment in the past that made little sense to him at the time.

"She's practically insane from the possession," Enon said calmly. "As I warned you, she will do anything to keep this demon."

"Think about how he behaves when he hasn't done an exorcism in a while. How does he behave after?" I petitioned, now searching Puck on my right for something resembling logic.

"She is drunk with my power," Enon said.

I looked back at Enon. "It's not really power, Enon. It's pure rage. The beast won't feed you. It will destroy you."

He leaned down and whispered in my ear. "Then why hasn't it destroyed you?" He stood back up and raised his hands ceremoniously. "Let's begin."

The question about my body's ability to withstand an extraneous soul and the weight of the beast's anger deserved an answer. Unfortunately, I didn't have one. I also didn't have enough time to figure it out. I was just starting my second—no wait—third exorcism this week, and I was a little pre-occupied with the battle going on inside of me.

As if being split three times, plus one, wasn't enough, Enon was trying to rip another piece away. If Paula was angry that I had left, she would be furious that Enon was stealing her favorite punching partner.

"You won't be allowed to kill me," I said over the chant of the coven. I glanced around at them. The words they were speaking differed from those of the sisters. I presumed it was the difference between homemade spells and prayers translated into Latin.

"I have no intention of killing you, Hennie. But I'm also not going to let you fall into the wrong hands."

"Wrong hands?" I chuckled, feeling an overwhelming pressure sink into my bones. I had underestimated the power in this little quartet. They packed a punch. I turned my head, observing the trail of glow sticks that were acting as the circle for this procedure. They were inventive, I'll give them that. And after my history, I had to respect fire safety.

I saw someone moving in the shadows beyond the circle. When he came into view, my mouth gaped. The tall, suited man paced inside the warbled line of magical influence. Not Paula playing the part of Paul, but my shadow. The man I only ever saw in my reflection. The sphere being created by the coven was shifting reality just enough to reveal him to my human eyes.

Just off to my left, still tucked behind my peripheral vision, was the twitch of a tail. The beast was not sentient by normal standards, but it sensed something was afoot. The only question was, should I let it come out and play—or should I try to hang onto it? I never was good at containing my anger. How was I supposed to keep a grip on a 600lb temper with claws and teeth?

"Better learn fast," my shadow answered my internal question.

Enon glanced over at the man within the circle. His jaw clenched, and he waved his hand over my face. "Blind." As soon as he said the word, I lost vision. "Deaf." I missed the wave of his hands, but I assumed it was there. Following his command, the world went silent. A slight ringing perhaps, but beyond that, nothing.

If I'm being completely honest, I rather enjoyed the break from monotone party chatter, but not seeing anything was a difficulty. I felt something slither up my arm. 15,000 undulating muscles dragged a tickling tongue up to my face. The serpent crossed my neck and positioned itself over the brand on my chest.

"See with my eyes. Hear with my ears." I couldn't hear the request with my ears, of course, just my mind. It was one of those many perks of sharing consciousness with another being. As with most things in my magic bag, I didn't know how to do what my shadow was asking, but he guided me. I felt him draw me up. Lifting me from my body as if I were having an out-of-body experience.

"Open."

I opened my eyes and blinked at myself lying on the table. I looked down at the suit I was wearing. I was him. I was the serpent. We had simply changed places.

Out-of-body experience indeed.

"Stop him." This time, the word wasn't his voice. It was mine. My catatonic body was speaking to me without moving its lips.

I ignored my questions about this transference. I assumed it wasn't a cheat, since binding with me was binding with him. I walked around the circle watching the coven doing their best to draw out the beast. I could see it in the corner now. Or at least as much as anyone could ever see it. The black skin only revealed itself with movement.

The cracks in the bends of its body exposed the molten lava within.

"How do I stop this?" There was no answer from my body. Either the serpent didn't know, or I couldn't say.

I paced the floor much as my shadow had just done. I searched my mind for the answer. I considered the risks of letting out the beast. I also considered the risk of putting the beast inside an already powerful demon. Enon may have claimed he had no designs to overtake the world, but that didn't mean the beast wouldn't want to take its revenge out against its least favorite species.

The beast shifted from the corner and sauntered over to Enon. The black cat stopped behind him and Enon smiled. Whatever he was doing was working. The beast was being lured in by his invitation. Under normal circumstances, I'd be thrilled to be rid of my pissy kitty cat, but there was no way outside of hell that Enon could tolerate the burden of that much emotion. Again, I confronted the question of my own continued sanity, but still had no answer. For now, I would assume Hennie's body was abnormally strong and could tolerate the beast.

As I looked around the coven, I thought of what was quite possibly the stupidest plan I had ever had in my life. My body blinked, and its head turned to frown at me. I shrugged in my Armani suit and my body rolled its eyes at me before settling back on the table. Nothing like getting flak from one's own body.

Despite the serpent's disapproval of my plan, I felt him concede. I watched the exorcism with interest. I felt Enon's anticipation rise as the beast got closer to him. He leered, pre-emptively satisfied with his imprudent actions.

I noticed that my body had also donned a smug little smirk.

At last, the beast reared. I felt it inside of me. It was ready to bolt. To run to greener pastures. Someplace it could frolic freely and share its parasitic ire. The moment the mammoth creature's claws dug into Enon's back, I grabbed onto Zeus and Vlad. The serpent reached out and touched Raven and Puck. The contact was far more metaphysical than literal, but the result was the same: a sudden, simultaneous shock.

For the first time since I discovered my power, I was working *with* my shadow. We were moving as one, thinking as one, and the beast instinctively followed suit.

Power-hungry and ready to have an endless supply of strength, Enon stupidly opened himself up to the beast—inviting him in. The others didn't understand. They didn't know he wasn't exorcising this so-called demon, but actually offering himself up as a vessel.

Opening yourself for possession, while dumb, was not nearly as idiotic as what I was about to do. I was going to become a possessor. And not just of Enon, because of course he wasn't only leaving himself open for possession. He was leaving his coven vulnerable as well.

No one ever reads the fine print of merging with a coven. If they did, they would realize it is effectively permissible possession. You share memories, emotions, and any tangible, unifiable power with the group. The fundamental difference between this witchery and a demonic possession is that a witch still has her original body to reside in. There is no embodiment. Plus, your fellow witches aren't being dicks to you.

Usually.

In the traditional merge, each member surrenders to the others, achieving an integrated coven. Of course, much like anything involving someone of greater strength, there is a nonconsensual version. The down-and-dirty version of a merging, for all intents and purposes, was basically mental rape. Since I was already connected to Enon, and he to the group, I could have categorized my actions as date rape. Regardless of what crime I compared it to, though, I was being a total asshole.

But Enon had been an asshole first.

My triple grip on the coven—beast, serpent, and soul—nearly overwhelmed them. They all gasped, including Enon, which I thought was a good sign. I pushed myself inside the link and, unlike Enon's filtered connection, I showed them everything.

Absolutely everything.

I remembered how in my link with Paula, she had shown me a lame backstory that, while perhaps true for someone, had been a ridiculous lie for the person she really was. Enon had done much the same. He'd perpetuated the image of a saint while he'd performed acts of cannibalism right under their noses.

As I pushed out my memories, the details of the coven's history trickled back into mine. I saw their lives one at a time. The misfit group of troubled youths had endured countless rejections and harbored genuine regrets for their vengeful thoughts and actions. On some level, I felt I belonged here with them, more so than with the sisters. Their pain seemed to match better with my own. Hopefully, that comparison drew on their sympathies.

My backstory unfolded as a normal girl with some unfortunate deaths to deal with. Then my interactions with the coven brought them the knowledge of my power. My power—not Enon's. Then things got messy. I could sense the confusion about my choices after leaving the coven. Their sympathy for me soured as they learned about the awful things I did under the devil's influence. The introduction of the beast had a ripple effect on the group. They knew it was inside of me. I was now no longer an innocent to them, but the vessel for a turbulence that didn't belong on Earth.

Just when I felt the coven band together to reject me, I revealed the rest of my story. My first meeting with Enon. The exorcism, the revelation about his identity and his proclivities. There was a collective pause and, either out of shock or despair, they released the pressure against me.

The link—forced though it was—solidified. I was now part of the coven.

That was where the stupidity lay. My temporary link with Enon would have dissolved if not for this permanent one. It was what he'd wanted all along, so he didn't fight to keep the beast with him.

In the short term, I had revealed Enon's true self to the coven, but I had also connected them to the beast. Even though I pushed it back, forcing it into a passive state, I felt its presence trickling into the link. All the hurt and pain life had thrown at this coven was coming to the surface like oil on water. All that was needed was a match.

The anger within them—the anger I had recognized as being similar to my own—was feeding the already tumultuous beast within me. That anger called to me. I wasn't sure why, but I laughed.

Not me-me—here in the serpent's form—but him-me, the serpent in my body. Watching myself laugh at their combined pain made me feel sick. There was no pleasure here. There was no entertainment.

I heard the beast roar in the corner, brought to life by the indignity of the serpent. I tried to push it back again, but it was fighting me much as I was fighting it. Force never worked with the beast. We were much too alike. That, in and of itself, pissed me off. I hated that I shared more parallels with a raging beast than any other facets of the devil. Not that I preferred to be a manipulative bitch, but still.

When I had nearly lost control of my own emotions and was moments from subjecting my poor mind-raped coven to the fury that had created hell, I remembered one of my very first acts as a coven member.

Love.

I had quelled the anger and pain of my fellow sisters. I had poured as much of myself into them as I could. Only the good stuff, of course. I had calmed them.

Unfortunately, my fuel gauge for love was running low. My thoughts of my childhood seemed distant and false to me now that Hennie was gone. My love for my coven was so tangled in resentment that it would only further draw out the beast. And Dane—God, how I wished I could focus on love when I thought of him, but now he was just a murderer again. A killer of women; a killer of me.

I didn't even consider Enon as a source. Talk about a doomed romance. Several times in his bed and twice on his table—this had to be my most subversive love connection yet.

That was it. I was all out of love.

Except for Jess.

My poor, sweet, kind of dingy but oh-so-much-fun Jess. She was right that it didn't matter how she died. I was still mad I couldn't stop it, but now for reasons of human failings, not magical ones.

I would give it up, I think. For her.

All of it. The magic. The power.

I would go back to the beginning and rewrite myself as a stupid, ignorant girl who got walked all over and never caught a break. I would do that for her, so I wouldn't have to be the angry one. So the devil wouldn't have lured me into an irrational attempted murder. So Sister Aggie didn't teach me and I could be a normal human. That was all I wanted, anyway.

For Jess, I would even give up Dane, Rachel, and the rest of the coven. She was worth losing them all. That's how much I loved her.

I felt that love spread over me. The fire in my veins that was making my heart thump cooled. It felt good to be able to do that still. It felt like there was the smallest chance I wasn't a monster.

When I closed my eyes and opened them again, I was back in my body again. Enon was smirking down at me. His coven was looking at him with horror, but he didn't care. He had what he'd wanted from me. The beast and my soul were now connected to the coven. I was a proper fuel source for them and him. The only advantage—as slight as it was—was that he didn't have shared control of my power anymore. Dispersed evenly among the group, he couldn't readily access it without the group being involved. That was a small, gambled victory.

"Thank you." Enon leaned down and kissed me. It was a hard kiss—the equivalent of a smack in the face, if you ask me. I bit his lip, but all I tasted was dirt, not blood.

When he leaned back, I saw Raven's face. The mixture of emotions there was understandable. She was in love with Enon, but he was far from being the "angel" she'd thought he was. Not only that, but she had just relived his carnal interactions with me. That would be enough to put any woman into *Fatal Attraction* territory.

She was panting, and her eyes were darting between me and him. I didn't react, and I certainly didn't attempt to calm her down. A single word out of my mouth might have resulted in an explosion of curses. Since Enon seemed absolutely ignorant to the poor girl grappling for her own sanity, he also said nothing.

It was the last straw and I could feel it. Even if the link between us hadn't made me acutely aware of her desperation for his love, I could see it all over her face. She had reached the *Glen Close* stage.

I didn't even know the knife was there until she grabbed it. The blood ritual must have required some kind of blade. However, the 6-inch hunter's knife was a little excessive. I gasped as it suddenly appeared and barreled down at my chest with murderous speed.

There was no time to react. The air I was gathering in my gasp was a fatal delay since I couldn't speak a word to stop her movement before the knife reached me. Since she was an innocent, the murder would be permissible. Hennie's body would die. I would return to hell and all my progress would be lost because of her.

Oh, God, please! Not her! Don't let Raven be the one that brings me down.

Even as the blade reached my chest, hands gripped Raven's, stopping her momentum and preventing my death. I looked over at Zeus, who was lying across me—having leaped forward to stop her. I only managed to catch a glimpse of his eyes before he looked at Raven.

His interference pissed her off. In fact, she was still trying to push the knife in. Between Zeus's tensed biceps and the lack of momentum, it was easily being repelled by my sternum. I was safe. However, the tip was cutting into my skin.

"Release," I said, remembering that I was not powerless.

Raven released the knife instantly and Zeus pulled it away from my breastbone.

"Cut!" Raven screamed at me—trying out a little taste of revenge, care of a foreign power in her blood. My cheek opened up, much as it had when I'd used the power on her. For a moment, the injury pleased her, but then Vlad pushed past her to rest his hand against my cheek. I hadn't expected him to heal me, given the circumstances, but I imagined he considered himself under a certain obligation to do so. A magical Hippocratic Oath, if you will.

Raven looked over her coven, searching for a friend to side with her anger. Puck was the only one not glaring at her, but he couldn't hold her gaze long enough to reassure her. Her face fell, and she ran from the room in tears. The worst of it was that I could feel her. I could feel the pain I was causing her—a torment mistresses rarely get to feel.

I looked down at Zeus as he cut away my restraints and tossed the knife away. He rubbed his eyes in frustration, no doubt overwhelmed by the revelations of the evening. When he looked up again, I caught his eye. He had been a mystery before, but now I could see into him. I could see his softness and bravery. I could see the path he'd almost taken. It was good that Enon had prevented it. Murder-suicide was never a good way to get revenge.

His gaze shifted to Enon. "You lied to us, you bastard."

"I never lied," Enon said, indifferent to the castigation. "You assumed, and I didn't correct you. You created this image. I merely maintained it for you."

"You really eat demons?" Vlad asked, appalled. I found some irony in this, since he was effectively playing the part of a vampire. Well, *playing* wasn't quite the right word for it since he actually used his fangs occasionally. However, he always healed his victims up afterward. He was definitely a weird cat, but in his world of vampire groupies, he was a god.

"I'll explain everything," Enon assured them.

"What's the point?" Puck said. "She already told us everything. You never would have told us otherwise."

Enon sighed. "Then there is nothing left to say." He walked away, but Puck and Zeus went after him. Zeus continued to berate him as they went, scolding him like an errant child. Even Puck was no longer kissing his ass. He jumped in with a few supplementary reprimands when needed.

Vlad moved to follow them, but stopped when I sat up. He looked down at the wound on my sternum. It wasn't deep since the knife had only penetrated skin deep, but during the struggle, the blade had dragged a little, making it a long cut rather than just the original puncture.

"You want me to take care of that?" he asked. He licked the tip of his crowned canine after he asked. I knew he wasn't asking to heal me. He wanted a taste.

This was his vampire act. It was definitely an act, but the strange thing was I understood why he did it. It had nothing to do with drinking blood. It was about his desire not to be human. To be something else. To be special in some way.

I wondered whether he would accept me more now, knowing I was, in fact, not human. The irony was that I wanted to be a boring human.

I chuckled at him. "Do you think I'll taste different?"

"Only one way to find out."

Just for kicks, I pulled the collar of my t-shirt down for him. He moved closer, but stopped in front of me. "What exactly are you anyway?" he asked before proceeding.

"What do you mean?"

"I mean, are you really a part of the devil?"

"I'm just his soul."

"Does that make you an angel?" he asked.

I barked out a laugh. "No. I think it makes me..." My mind scrambled to find a description. "A blank slate."

"You don't seem blank to me." He narrowed his eyes at me as if he were reading me right then and there. "You seem like a woman that has been written on all of her life. People telling her what to do, what to feel, and how to behave."

"Sounds like I'm human then."

"Yeah, but it also sounds like you've forgotten to write on yourself. You need to be who you want to be. Not who everyone is telling you you are."

"Is that what you do?"

Vlad nodded and leaned forward, licking the blood from my wound. The proximity to my cleavage should have made it feel sensual, but it didn't. It felt oddly cat-like and mothering. There was a slight tingling in his contact, and when he leaned back, I saw the wound had mended.

"Do I… taste different?" I asked, now concerned that perhaps my origins would somehow influence my very blood.

"Yes," Vlad said grimly. "You taste like barbecue."

It took me a second longer than I would like to admit to realize he was teasing me.

I snorted and laughed. I even went so far as to nudge his shoulder playfully.

He smirked at me and motioned me to the door. "Come on, she-devil. Let's go kick Enon's lying ass."

CHAPTER 29

As if my life wasn't messed up already, I was now permanently linked to a man willing to take on the entirety of the devil's anger simply because he was peckish. Enon may have been living as a human, but that didn't make him humane. Everything he did was to support his own appetite—be it hunger or lust. Despite being a member of this coven, he had no true loyalties to anyone.

When Enon had had enough of his coven lecturing him, he left the bar altogether. I followed him out of the building and stalked him down the sidewalk. It was early morning, and the sun was peeking over the horizon, but not the buildings yet. The chill in the air wasn't quite enough to send me running for a jacket, but close.

"What the hell were you thinking?" I yelled after him.

His head shifted, acknowledging I was there. "You know what I was thinking."

"Do you think this is a game?" I asked. "Do you think playing with this kind of power is just a Sunday drive?"

Enon stopped and lowered his head. I could hear the perturbed rasp in his exhale. "Do you have any idea what it's like to have a two-year-old brandishing a finger at you?" Enon turned his condescension on me. He moved back and slowly pressed his hand to my chest. The brand was gone, obliterated by a stronger connection. The draw that came with it was gone, too. I still felt him inside me—that dull earthly pressure that felt neither good nor evil—but the coven had dispersed it.

Enon pushed against me, shoving me back into the brick building we were walking past. I tried to shove him back, but his weight was not muscle and bone. I didn't bother reaching for my magic since it would only provoke him to use his too, and I already knew how that would go.

"I've been honest about my intentions, Hennie. I was not going to wait for your sisters to pay you another visit and take what's mine."

"I don't belong to you."

"I don't give a shit about you. All I ever wanted from you was the power inside of you. And now I have it. And I'm never letting it go."

I remembered what my shadow had said about Enon. How I wouldn't be able to break free of him. How the only option for survival would be extracting him from the Earth. I also remembered thinking such an exorcism would be nearly impossible. Enon had effectively been possessing the earth for a thousand years. How does one begin to break apart that bond?

Enon clucked his tongue at me. "I can see those wheels turning. Don't even think about it, Hennie. Your coven has been filling you with delusions of grandeur, but it's a waste of your time to come after me. You may be the devil—or part of him—but... well..." He tapped my head. "You're broken, aren't you?" He moved his hand to my cheek and dragged his thumb along my lower lip. His eyes focused on my mouth like he was about to kiss me. "So, until you learn how to be the devil, then you can consider me the second most powerful being ever in existence." He moved away, skipping the rest of the seduction that usually ended with me in his bed.

I laughed—a somewhat fake display, just to get his attention. This was the part of me I truly hated. The little voice inside of me that demanded I get the last word. It was the reason I'd spent so much time getting into fights during school. It was the reason Rachel and I had such a volatile relationship. I imagined it had something to do with why I couldn't fully admit to myself that I loved Dane.

Enon stopped in his tracks. He may have been a demon, but he had spent enough years as a human to lose his immunity to mockery. I waited for him to turn so he could see my smirking face.

"You're nothing, Enon. You aren't human. You aren't sanctified. You're a freeloader." I moved toward him, flaunting my smack talk. Perhaps I could raise my maturity level in his eyes to teenage status. "Why do you think you've been here for a thousand years?" I looked around as if I might find the answer within the mortar of the brick building. "Oh, right, because no one cares." I said the words slow and loud so he could understand them better. "You're still here because you are of no consequence to this world." I pushed into his chest, practically begging for my ass-kicking. "I may be a broken shell of the devil with no memory, but you are just a piece of dirt. And as soon as I figure out how, I'm going to scrape you off the bottom of my shoe."

I brushed past him to walk on. I was rather pleased with my moment. More pleased that Enon hadn't tried to punch me or put me in a headlock. Maybe he really was more mature than me.

"Is that before or after your apocalypse kills all of your friends?"

My feet slowed to a stop against my will. I didn't want to stop. I wanted to walk away in my huff, the winner of the verbal riposte. But there was no lie in his proposed scenario. I turned back and glared at him. "I thought the apocalypse was an everyday event. Nothing to worry about. Isn't that what you said?"

Enon smiled at me, pleased that he had baited my thirst for information. "I don't think I ever said that. I rarely worry about the apocalypses because—as you said—I'm usually insignificant to their cause and unaffected by the reset." Enon sauntered up the sidewalk and stopped a few feet from me. He crossed his arms and rubbed his chin. "Don't worry, I'm sure you'll only kill a few thousand people before he intervenes." I blanched at that number. "Oh, shit, you thought resetting meant that no one would die? My mistake. It's usually a hurricane in these parts. Some natural event to explain the devastation at the epicenter." I swallowed, searching for a question, but not finding anything. "Yeah, sorry about the confusion. I didn't mean to suggest that you causing an apocalypse wouldn't be damaging to anyone—just not *everyone*."

He moved forward, but stopped next to me. "I don't want to control you, Hennie. I'm perfectly happy to let you live your life—your sanctified, human life—however you please. But I will give you some advice."

I refused to turn and look at him, but I stayed quiet, giving him permission to condescend even though I really wanted to punch him in the face.

"Maybe you should accept the protection my free-loading hunger provides. Because picking a fight with me will definitely bring you that much closer to self-destruction." He paused, allowing me time to retort if I wanted, but I had nothing left to say. I felt a warble of his power flow through me as he walked away. It was the equivalent of a magical muscle flex.

The insult made the beast inside of me rear and growl, but I took a steadying breath and mentally shushed it. There was no point in getting angry now. I had put myself into this trap to protect the world from the beast. I had succeeded in that. Maybe Enon was right; maybe I needed to accept that this was my new normal. I had a new coven and a new ex-boyfriend to resent with all of my heart. Everything was going to be okay.

I walked on and turned the corner of the building. As if karma was bitch-slapping me, I ran right into Rachel.

CHAPTER 30

A LIFETIME IN A moment was the saying, but it was never truer than when I was standing there staring into Rachel's eyes. She looked dumbfounded—no doubt shocked that she had simply stumbled upon me. I knew my face was registering a level of fear I had never known before.

Where had she come from? How had she found me? But of course, I answered my own question the moment I'd asked it. Joining with the coven must have lit me up like a damn beacon. Even if Dane wasn't a bloodhound and even if the coven wasn't on high alert, Paula would have sensed this shift in power like a poke in the eye.

Rachel should have called out to the coven. I could see them meandering around down the street, popping in and out of stores, searching for me. It was the worst game of hide-and-seek ever. All Rachel had to do was yell at them or reach out with her magic, but she didn't. She remained frozen.

I didn't dare move. Like a wild animal, she would pounce the moment she sensed my escape. So, I just stared back at her.

Tears sprung to her eyes, and she swallowed hard. I could see her eyes flitting as if she wanted to look behind her—to see who was close enough to call out to. She still didn't do it. I knew she was struggling with this path. Being a killer was not what nuns did. She had joined the convent to punish her murderous hand and now, here she was, raising her scythe again.

I felt my own eyes water. A reaction to her emotions, I told myself. I shouldn't have been crying. I should have been screaming at her and hitting her. Where was the beast now? Why was it quiet while I stared into the face of my killer? Why was I crumbling instead of burning? I was the devil, dammit. The devil doesn't cry!

After what seemed like forever, I couldn't take it anymore. "Do it," I whispered. "Call them. Or would you prefer to do it yourself?" I pulled back my t-shirt, allowing her plenty of room to slit my neck if she wished to.

Rachel looked over my neck. She shook her head as a tear spilled from her eyes. "Hennie—"

"Hey!" Ruby yelled from across the street. I barely had time to look before a massive burst of energy hit me like a punch.

My body went clean through the wall I hit, leaving me in a heap of debris on the other side. The beauty shop patrons I had nearly crashed into looked at me fearfully as I got my aching body out of the mess. I glanced through the hole and saw Rachel still staring back at me. Still not attacking me. If this was her idea of a cat batting at a mouse, she was soon going to figure out that I was no mouse.

"Hennie, wait—" Rachel started, but I was in no mood to listen. I threw back my version of a magical punch. She barely cleared the opening in time and my stinging pain bomb landed on Ruby instead. Her rush to get across the street halted as she dropped to the road, screaming in pain.

Rachel looked from Ruby to me. There was a certain disappointment there, as if she knew that little spell had been formulated just for her—a very long-awaited slap in the face I hadn't quite managed to get in before my prior escapes.

"Stay away from me!" I seethed and ran toward the nearest exit.

"Hennie!" Rachel yelled after me, but I didn't wait or slow my escape. I had an entire coven searching the neighborhood for me, and my chances of avoiding a fight were based solely on the speed of my human legs.

I found an exit leading to a courtyard. As impressed as I was by this city's desire to maintain natural spaces within the brick-and-mortar terrain, it was really starting to piss me off.

I ducked into the adjacent building, which turned out to be a restaurant. I got more than a few stares as I passed by the tables of early bird diners. I couldn't blame them. I was in my pajamas and powdered white with drywall dust. In another city, I may have passed as an art installation, but so far no one was buying my interpretation of a living statue.

I pushed out the front door to the sidewalk.

"Here! Here!" Kate yelled from down the block. "The devil has wings!"

I bolted across the street, ignoring more of Kate's rants, which I thought only occasionally made sense. I followed the sounds of music down into an obscure bar. The red walls reminded me of hell, though I was certain I didn't actually have a memory of it. The band on stage was mostly just doing a soundcheck since the only bar-hoppers weren't hopping so much as camping out. I ran toward what I thought was an exit, but it only turned out to be the bathrooms.

"Fan out! Find her!" Paula's voice sounded like nails in a coffin to me.

I moved back out of the hall to get to the other branch, which might lead to an exit. The telltale red letters of my escape put hope back into my heart, but Meredith's entrance doused my excitement. She immediately started searching the rooms on her way. Janitor's closet, coat room, and then she would find me.

I backed down the bathroom hall, contemplating how I could get out of this without killing anyone. Some part of me knew Paula would stop at nothing to get what she wanted. The only thing more dangerous than the devil was the devil with human survival instincts. The only way to get her out of my hair was to eliminate her bloodhounds.

Which one?

I could hear Meredith pushing through the racks in the coatroom. Would she be the first? Could I actually kill her to save myself?

No.

I felt my body sag as I once again felt the morality of my soul put me back into the line of fire. I wanted to live, but not at anyone's expense. If it really came to that, I would willfully die.

Too bad I couldn't take Paula down with me.

I tensed as footsteps neared the entrance to the hall. I held up my hands, prepared to surrender myself. Meredith rounded the corner. When her eyes met mine, she smiled and entered the women's restroom.

I heard the doors to the stalls being kicked open before she returned to the hall. She walked right past me and into the men's restroom. She gave the stalls the same treatment, checking every inch of space, including the lock on the window, before returning to the corridor.

She paused at her exit and looked back at me. "You haven't seen a woman come through here, have you? Long blond hair with black tips and a nose ring?"

I stared at Meredith, trying to figure out what she was playing at. I didn't dare speak, so I shrugged limply and shook my head. Satisfied with my answer, she headed further in to check the kitchen.

Befuddled by my narrow and miraculous escape, I took a step forward to check my appearance in a mirrored sconce on the wall. I couldn't see all of me, but I was clearly an elderly woman with an unappealing number of skin tags on my neck. It not only looked real, but I could feel the wrinkled skin on my face. Even the pain in my hip seemed to be from sciatica instead of my recent trip through a wall.

"Come with me," Zeus said from the head of the corridor.

I turned to him, impressed and grateful for his critical timing.

"Hurry, this is difficult for me."

I nodded and followed his lead out of the hall. Despite my preference for using the back door, I sensed the makeshift magical alarm Meredith had put up. If I left that way, it would draw attention. Attention Zeus's tenuous skills may not overcome.

Zeus moved across the bar at a slow, intentional pace. He obviously didn't want to draw attention by running for his life. Nor did I, so I moved as slowly as I thought an 80-year-old might. It was surreal walking through a room with my enemies so close and not attacking me. The steady beat of the drummer helped me keep my pace despite my heart thumping several times faster.

The keyboardist chimed in, marking the moment I saw Dane searching behind the bar. The owner was nearly ready to pick a fight with him, but Dane just shoved him aside and pushed through.

I glanced over when the singer started his solemn song. It was beautiful, to be sure, but it was the lyric about teaching the devil to fly that caught my attention. I saw Kate standing right at the edge of the stage, waving her head around to the music. The musician wasn't in the least fettered by a nun dancing to his devilish tune. He even removed the microphone and leaned down to sing directly to her.

Halfway to the exit, I spotted Paula coming back down from her upstairs search. She looked furious. It was the first time I had seen her looking less than gorgeous. She had dark bags under her bloodshot eyes, and her skin no longer glowed. Her darkness was showing through, I thought.

She crossed the bar ahead of Zeus and blocked his path out of the bar. She pressed her finger into his chest, making him flinch. "Have you seen her?"

"Who?" Zeus asked.

"Have you seen a young blond girl in here?" she asked.

Shit! I saw the tactic, but I couldn't warn Zeus without revealing us both. All I could do was hope he knew the most important rule in hell's playbook. Don't lie to the devil!

Zeus shook his head, and I cringed. "No, I haven't."

I didn't hear the lie. I wasn't sure that could be right unless Zeus had changed me before he ever saw me. He wasn't lying. He was safe.

I, on the other hand...

Zeus continued on and I followed—right into the path of danger. Paula was so close I could smell the spark of flint on her. She eyeballed me carefully, noting my limp and distinct facial aberrations. "What about you, ugly old bat?"

I sniffed and wiped my nose, before waving her away like I expected an old woman might if you insulted her to her face. I tried to walk past her, but Paula raised her arm to block me.

"Have you seen a girl come through this bar?"

I considered my answer as well. Since I was that girl, I couldn't have seen myself. And when I had seen myself, I was under this spell, so technically I wouldn't be lying either. However, I didn't know if this spell included a voice? I looked at Zeus, poised at the door, ready to leave. He gave me a nod, and I spoke.

"I haven't theen—" I gagged as something pushed forward in my mouth. Paula's face crinkled with disgust. I reached up to touch whatever I had vomited through my lips and found teeth. Dentures. My dentures had come out of my mouth. I laughed out loud, unable to quell my amusement.

"Uck! Get out of here, old woman!"

I shoved my dentures back into place and headed out the door with Zeus.

CHAPTER 31

A s soon as we were out the door, Zeus fell against the brick wall and panted like he had run a mile in concrete shoes. "I'm sorry," he rasped. "I can't hold it any longer."

"You did fine," I assured him. I leaned forward and pressed a grateful kiss to his lips. When I drew back, he looked well beyond shocked and into terrified. "That one was for you," I said.

He swallowed hard and nodded. "Thank you," he whispered.

"Come on, let's keep moving." I urged him to keep going, even though he was exhausted. "How did you find me?" I asked once we were around the next block and away from the coven.

"We all sensed you were in danger. I found you first, I guess."

"Well, I'm glad you did, but I'm not out of danger yet. Dane will track me down if I don't get some distance between us."

"Dane?"

"My ex."

"The big guy behind the bar?"

"Yeah."

"Oh." Zeus sounded a little pouty. "But that's over, right?" he asked eagerly.

I stopped and looked at him. "Why does it matter?" I asked, instantly regretting the pity kiss I had given him.

"I just thought maybe when things go south with Enon, you and I—"

"*When* things go south? Not *if*?"

"Come on." Zeus shrugged. "Don't be like Raven. You know he's got like ten other covens." I frowned at this new knowledge. Enon may not have been connected to the coven prior to my interference, but that didn't mean some of his secrets weren't already out. "He moves from city to city. This is the first we've seen of him in months. If you think he doesn't have a dick sucker in every one of those covens, you're wrong. He's a total player. He will never be anybody's boyfriend."

This assessment did not surprise me, nor did it hurt me. I had long since eliminated Enon as a candidate for hand-holding and cuddling. "But you would? You would be my boyfriend?"

"I..." Zeus's voice broke. "I would be everything for you. I would do anything."

I stared at him in stunned silence. This was not the time or place to be having this conversation, but his effort impressed me. "But I'm the devil."

"You have a good heart," he said earnestly. "I could see that even before you merged with us. You deserve someone who can bring you joy."

"Wow, that is the sweetest thing any man has ever said to me. And possibly the most incorrect. Let me save you some trouble for the future. I don't have a good heart. I'm actually a bitch." I grabbed his hand. "Now we need to—"

"Hennie!" Dane's voice called out to me.

He was on the opposite end of the block, staring back at me. I couldn't see him well enough to know if he was glaring or not, but I certainly was. I was still fuming about everything that had happened. He'd effectively baited me into Rachel's trap. They had almost succeeded in killing me.

"Don't run," he warned.

"I won't," I said, and I didn't. I reached my clawed hand out Darth Vader-style and closed it around an imaginary larynx. Dane reached for his neck, playing the part of Admiral Motti very well. I wasn't sure I wanted to kill him, merely give him a taste of his own medicine.

"No, let's go!" Zeus tugged at my hand, disrupting my concentration and releasing Dane. He dragged me into an alley on the other side of the street. There was no point in disguising me now. They had spotted Zeus and the coven would add him to the list of my accomplices.

"Go on without me."

"What? No!" He squeezed my hand. "I'll get you out of here."

"Psst!" Raven hissed from above us on the roof.

I looked up at her frantic come-hither hand gesture. I pulled my hand from Zeus's grip. "Go, now!" I insisted, ready to trade one protector for another. I leaped up the fire escape with speed that competed with my high school track days. When I reached the top, I looked back at Zeus. He was waiting at the end of the alley to make sure I had gotten up safely. It was sweet, but...

Crap, what had I started?

"There he is!" Dane announced as he hit the alley with Rachel, Meredith, and Lynn.

I ducked back, narrowly avoiding being seen. I crouched down slowly, keeping my feet from making a noise against the gravelly roof. I heard footsteps as Dane ran down the alley to catch Zeus. With any luck, he would be a German Shepherd before Dane rounded the corner.

I caught Raven's eye across from me and I recognized the look on her face. We were alone. Zeus was gone, so there would be no witness to how this event went down.

I could see the plot forming in her mind. I was certain she could stand up and point to get the dirty deed done. Then she wouldn't have any competition for Enon. She could suck his dick all the livelong day without interference. Until he went on the road again.

If I could have raised a finger and gutted her like a fish, I would have. I knew my expression was telling her as much. But I couldn't and she knew that, too. I waited for the bitch to do it. I waited to see her smug face when she revealed my location. That was when I would release the beast and sink my claws into her like a gazelle on the Serengeti.

"Check the roof!" Rachel demanded below.

The sound of feet pounding up the fire escape disrupted my concentration on murderous and potentially carnivorous thoughts. I looked back to Raven to see if she intended to help me, but her glare had only changed to a smug satisfaction. I was ready to begin the gutting process, but Meredith yelled down to Rachel from her position on the stairs. She must have been almost to the top, judging by her voice.

"She didn't come this way without her magic. The last flight is missing." Meredith's feet pounded again—this time on her way down.

Raven's eyes gleamed with pride. She had opted to spare my life for the sake of the high road. In this case, the high road was effectively her saving me with the power I had recently made fun of.

When the coast was clear, we made our way down to ground level and started backtracking to keep Dane guessing. I wasn't sure what mechanism allowed him to find me, but I wouldn't assume keeping my magic off would restrict his abilities.

Unfortunately, my bright idea to backtrack was a colossal mistake, since half the coven was still behind me.

CHAPTER 32

THE WILD WEST WOULD be an excellent analogy, except I wasn't in a one-street town. I was surrounded by streets and alleys, rooftops and sewers galore. Lots of nooks to hide in, but too much space to escape from.

I wasn't sure who saw me first—Paula at the far end of the street, Dane through the alley, or maybe it was Rachel coming around the corner of the next block. Either way, hunters and a very long apartment building blocked me in. I didn't have to check the front door to know it was locked. Even if it hadn't been, I suspected there was a courtyard on the other side of it and not a back door as I wanted. Fucking green spaces.

"It's over, Hennie. We won't let you go again," Paula yelled as she strutted down the street to me.

"Paula!" Rachel yelled back at her. "Let me talk to her."

"I've had enough talk. This little bitch is going back to where she belongs once and for all!"

Paula threw a spell at me. Instead of protecting myself as I should have, I used my power to push Raven clear of the blast. I expected to feel pain or emotional torment, but this little bullet was something more familiar. The lure of my old power attached itself to me. The familiar exhilaration hit me like a drug to a long-cured addict. As much as I didn't want it, I keeled to its will, drinking in every last sip of it, like a glass of water in the middle of the desert.

"There you are," my shadow's voice called to me. I crawled forward to see myself in the reflection of a small puddle. I could see my eyes were black with the oily control of hell's tainted magical flow. My shadow wasn't standing over me as I expected. It was only me—black-eyed me. "It still feels good, doesn't it?" my reflection asked. "I still feel good." I watched my face speak to me as if it were a separate entity.

"Yes," I admitted.

"Stop this, Paula," Rachel yelled back at her. "This isn't what we agreed to."

"You agreed to help me stop her. This is how we stop her," Paula said. "Now step aside."

"No," Rachel said.

I looked up to see if Rachel's face was as determined as her voice. She was standing not far from me in the middle of the street. Her coven had convened with her, standing in a line that occupied the width of the road. However, they weren't staring at me. They were looking at Paula.

I turned back and saw Paula arrive at my back. She was looking at Rachel with contempt. There was a rift forming between them. This cooperative effort to find me had taken its toll on both of them, no doubt the reason Rachel had attempted to put me down herself. She was trying a more humane approach. Something Paula didn't care one iota about.

It wasn't shocking to see them arguing. However, it surprised me it was taking precedence over my capture. I was incapacitated. The coven should have been surrounding me. They should have begun their exorcism. Not that they could remove me from this body now. I had the weight of the world pinned to my ass in the form of a dickhead risen.

"I won't let you kill her!" Rachel yelled.

She wouldn't?

Glaring white power flared all around Rachel as she spoke. Even through my smothering blanket of hell, I could feel her. She was magnificent. I didn't really know where my power landed on the spectrum of purity, but I knew she was the real deal.

In turn, each of the coven members put out their own flare until they looked like a line of white fire. I felt a little pang of envy at that moment. There had been no cool light shows when I was in the coven. Just inky black eyes and worried stares.

Paula laughed at their display. "We don't have time for this. The beast is inside of her. She—"

"The beast you put there," Rachel snapped.

"I had no choice. Giving Hennie a voice was my only chance to get her out willingly. That chance has come and gone. Our only option is to kill her. It has to be one of you. It has to be an innocent. Her death will stop the apocalypse."

"So will yours!" I managed to voice with enough clarity to participate in the conversation. I looked at Rachel, who was dipping her brow at this revelation. "The creation of the trinity was the first rip. I just made it worse. If you really want to prevent an apocalypse, then kill both of us. Paula and I will go back to hell and I'll take the beast with me." I felt claws dig into my back, making me wince. Apparently, the beast didn't like my plan. I wasn't the only one that didn't want to be caged up again.

"Is that what he told you?" Paula asked.

"He told me you will do anything to maintain your human form. That's why you are so desperate to get me back to where I belong. Before Daddy has to step in and fix it."

Paula smiled. "Interesting. He's helping you. I wonder. Did he ever tell you what *his* motivations were to get you back?"

I narrowed my eyes at her smug features. She had a secret to tell and she couldn't wait to tell me. I felt a tingle on my hand and looked down at the puddle I had peered into. My head was shaking. "Don't listen to her," my shadow's voice hissed through my teeth. "Destroy her while you still have the chance. Use my power and yours. Draw from the risen if you have to. Just eliminate her and we can be free!"

"I can't," I said. "He won't let me kill her."

"Think about it, Hennie." Paula sauntered forward, drawing the attention of the coven, but Rachel didn't attack. She seemed just as interested in this conversation as I was. "When we split, I took the physical form and placed myself here on Earth. To observe humanity and entertain myself with their delusions. I removed the beast out of necessity. We were going insane with all the rage inside of us. So off it went on its own, to smolder and burn, only popping up when we needed a good scare.

"All that was left was our mind and soul. The guiding force of our very existence. Without it, I'm just a shell and the beast would cease to exist. Then, of course, our story took a turn for the worse. You left and took on a human form. Much like me, you took on the characteristics of humanity. You eat and sleep as a human. You bond with others as a human."

"What's your point?"

"My point is, you idiot, you didn't take your mind with you. You ran off with the soul and left your brain behind. It was effectively self-induced amnesia. You disconnected yourself from your own reality. A vacation from yourself, if you will. Except the vacation turned into a more permanent engagement. While you were intentionally living life unaware of who you really were, we were working to jog your memory. To bring your mind and soul back together again. It took us a long time to get you to tread into a place of darkness. Someplace that would remind you of who you really are. It was just a sliver of an opening, but we took it. We helped your powers emerge in the hope that you would remember where you belonged. If you had, your mind and soul would merge once again. And perhaps it would have in time, but then Dear Ole Dad stepped in and sanctioned your existence—effectively limiting our capacity to get you back into your right state of mind."

I glanced at Rachel to see what she thought of this. She shifted her gaze to me, but it wasn't sympathy I saw there. It was worry. She didn't understand any more than I did why God would allow me to stay in this body—especially after the true soul had left. And like me, the unknown was more frightening to her than the known.

"Why did he want me back so bad?" I asked.

"Until now, you have been suppressing the memories of your true self. Denying your true existence. However, the longer you stay here, the closer you get to erasing your past altogether. Your human fantasy is starting to become a reality."

"Why does that even matter? Ignorance is bliss, isn't it?"

"Certainly, but if you forget who you are, the devil will cease to exist."

I blinked at her. "How can the devil cease to exist?"

"Easily. He is the second most powerful being in existence. He can do whatever he wants—as long as *God* allows it." Paula bit her simpering lips.

As long as God allows it?

As long as God allows it, I can cease to exist?

God has allowed me to stay, so I can assist in my own demise.

I felt a stinging pain in my back as razor-sharp claws dug into my flesh. A wave of heat trickled over my skin—effectively burning off the oily tracks of hell's tentacles. I felt the weight of the beast climbing onto my shoulders, but I didn't care. It pressed down on me until the weight of my hands cracked the concrete beneath me. Between the lumps of the road, I could see a slight glow, as if there was a fire starting in the ground below.

The weight of this ancient anger should have shattered me, but deep inside, the cool power of my soul shifted into my chest, making my heart ache and putting strength back into my limbs.

"That's why he let me stay," I whispered to myself as I got off the ground. I could feel the wind pick up around me, blowing dust into a vortex. "His ultimate plan..." I looked at Rachel for confirmation. "...was to facilitate my undoing." I didn't really recognize my voice. It wasn't the shadow or anything manly—just a little deeper and resonant than I thought I should have been capable of producing with human vocal cords.

Rachel frowned and shook her head. She had no more answers than me, but she was a dutiful representative of God and she didn't want to think He was capable of such an underhanded play. Fighting evil was what she did. It's what I'd thought I was doing, but as it turned out, I was only fighting myself. My fight to maintain my life here on Earth was cleaning up God's biggest mistake.

"He wasn't trying to save me." An impermissible tear dribbled down my cheek. Wasn't I clear about this? The devil doesn't cry! "He was eliminating me!" My voice boomed and lightning struck the road not far behind Paula. The thunder that coincided with the strike shook the ground like a slight earthquake.

"Hennie, stay calm," Rachel called to me.

"He wanted to get rid of me, just like you did," I seethed, relating this anger to every pain I had ever felt in my life. Every punch in the face. Every slur. I exhumed each minor offense down to the very last mosquito bite and filed it under the category of worthy-of-hell's-fury.

I looked down at Rachel and the other members of the coven. They were tensed and ready for battle. The expressions on their faces were a mixture of fear and awe. It took me a moment to recognize their craned necks as a sign of my height. I was floating above them.

I turned my attention to the storefront on the other side of the street. The tall windows that offered a glimpse at the merchandise inside were also giving me a glimpse of myself. The fiery light around me was far from the beautiful luminescence I saw in the coven. Bright red waves of energy completely obscured the watery blue in my chest. Jutting from my back were two long, transparent appendages. Remnants of a divergent form.

I was a monster.

I was the devil.

CHAPTER 33

T HE CONCRETE BENEATH ME groaned and cracked as the ground uprooted itself. The street pushed up and opened like a flower. The rock petals expanded and fell back, exposing a chasm. The bright glow of lava flowed up, forcing everyone to surrender the front line.

The heat was intense, but it was nothing compared to the fire pumping through my veins. I wanted to hurt Him. My creator. The Creator. I wanted to punch a hole through his beautiful little canvas and I was succeeding.

The street continued to fracture and fragment. Parts were pushing up, while others were sinking and melting into the Earth's blood. I was vaguely aware of what I was doing. I hadn't thought about the apocalypse as anything other than nuclear devastation or humans being chased by zombies. But that was just war and black Friday at Wal-Mart. That wasn't what caused an apocalypse.

An apocalypse was just as Paula had described it. The barrier between worlds was ripping away. The wall separating humans from the demons was crumbling.

That was why I was so dangerous. My anger held the power to construct hell.

And now, in light of this new treachery, I was going to expand my real estate.

With the help of the beast, I was opening a gateway right here and building a bridge between the two realms.

I was barely aware of myself now. I could feel something inside of me—beyond the risen, beyond the beast. I felt the sinuous tracks of muscle curling around my neck, pressing into my throat much as Dane had when he was strangling me. But at the moment, it didn't matter if I could breathe or not.

I could see Rachel watching me. Her eyes were registering so many emotions it was hard to keep track of what she was expressing. Fear, sadness, contempt, and guilt. She was regretting not killing me now. The trigger was always easier to pull when the enemy was charging.

I dared a glance at Dane and found similar sentiments. But there was something there I didn't expect. Relief? Was he grateful it was finally over? No more fighting, just a good hard wallop on the ass care of God himself.

Speaking of... Where was He? Wasn't someone going to stop me from destroying the Earth?

No?

How disappointing.

I sucked in a breath and raised my hands or claws or wings—or whatever the hell they were—so I could land a devastating blow. A tidal wave of horror was about to roll across the surface of the land and crumble anything in its path. It would have been beautiful.

"Haven't you ever wondered why I can see your shadow?" Enon called over to me above the din of roiling lava.

I stopped what I was doing and looked over at him. He was sitting on a concrete stoop in front of one of the apartment buildings. Not sitting—lounging. He was calm and relaxed. Uncaring.

Even above the rage that was already boiling inside of me, I still found room to hate him for that. His calm demeanor was proof that he was an even bigger asshole than me. I may have been ready to destroy the world, but he was the one sitting on the sidelines—watching it happen with a bucket of fucking popcorn in his lap.

I tried to whip a ball of fire at his head, but he batted it away using my power. It was like fighting with the beast. Fire against fire and whatnot. It was just annoying.

"Easy now, you don't want to hurt anyone," he said.

That was when I noticed my coven crouched down beside the stoop, all four of them huddled in a ball. The words they were speaking were calling to me in the very back of my mind. My connection to the coven was strong, but I was ignoring them. Just as I ignored the anchor they were putting on my power.

It wasn't enough to stop me. Not really.

They were reins on a horse, that was all. I could still run and buck and jump if I wanted. Most wild things are only tame if they choose to be. And even then, they can still change their minds.

Me being connected to them was no different from Paula being connected to Rachel's coven. They couldn't control her and if she wished it, she could control them. But those were old games for her.

Enon snapped his fingers as if I were an errant dog getting into the trash. "Did you hear me?" he asked. I got the sense he was drawing my attention away from my misfit coven. Drawing my fire—as it were.

"Why were you able to see my shadow?" I asked, since he seemed to think it was pertinent. I still sounded strange, but this time I was almost robotic. Like every emotion, including the anger, had evaporated in proximity to the beast's heat.

Enon smiled. He was enjoying this. Bastard.

He tapped his chest. "The bond. You and I were bonded together. I could feel you. I can still feel you, though not as well as I could when it was just the two of us."

I wanted to roll my eyes. Of course, it was the brand that had joined us and allowed him to see the serpent. Who seriously gives a crap about the details of the magic? Just let me get on with the breaking and the burning.

"You still don't get it yet, do you?" he asked, biting his lip. "She just told you." Enon motioned to Paula.

"Let it be, risen!" Paula warned him and threw a magical bolt at him. As with my attack, he veered it off with a raise of his hand.

"The mind, the soul, the body, and the fury." Enon listed off the entourage on his fingers. "The mind can't sustain without the soul. The body can't survive without the soul. And without the mind, the anger will extinguish."

I flinched as the beast pressed down on me, digging in its claws. It roared inside of me and I cried out partially from pain and partially to vent its anger. My anger.

I looked up at Enon, opened my mouth, and said, "Fuck you." The words were breathy and haunting—and not mine. I pressed my hand to my neck, feeling the scales that were slowly choking me. Cutting off my air and manipulating my voice. I didn't know where the serpent ended and I began.

Enon just smiled at my predicament. "Everyone's in a tizzy now, aren't they?" He jumped up and rubbed his hands together. "The whole trinity." Enon sucked in a breath and shook his head. "But it's not a trinity anymore, is it? I guess quartet doesn't sound as cool."

I wanted to scream at Enon to get on with it. Tell me what I needed to know. My interest in wreaking havoc on the world was dissipating, but only because I wanted to know what the hell he was trying to say. I could feel my misfits trying to reach me. They were little whispers in the dark—so frightened. They weren't so much trying to stop my power as pull on my pant leg. They were like little insistent children begging their mommy for a lollipop. Annoying, but adorable enough to be considered a persuasive force.

"Okay, let's try this again. Why can I see your shadow?" Enon asked.

"Because..." I croaked. "The link."

"The link to you." Enon jabbed his finger at me. He wasn't close enough to poke my forehead, but I could still feel it. "The link to your soul. Your body."

"Me," I said the word, but it was meaningless. Yes, me. And my shadow was a part of me or I was part of him—the definition was so dizzying that I had long since stopped trying to explain it even to myself.

"Who are you?" Enon yelled at me across the distance between us and inside of my mind.

"I'm... the devil," I answered with a hint of shame. It was the first hint of humanity I had shown since I broke a hole in the earth.

"That's who they want you to be," Enon said, pacing the bottom step. The lava was still steadily encroaching on his safe island. I got the sense from his uneasy glances that he was not immune to it. Because it wasn't just lava—it was liquid hell. It was the realm he had worked so hard to get out of, and so long to stay out of. Soon he would either have to grow wings or climb the building. "They want things to go back to the trinity. Why?"

"Because otherwise we'll die." I had spoken the words, and they were not nearly as foreign to me as the other things I had said, but I could hear the lie in them. It made no sense since I didn't require any special skill to detect my own lies. I already knew when I was lying, didn't I? Or in this case, perhaps I was lying to myself.

I turned my head to Paula, who was balancing on a jagged uprooted piece of road. She caught my gaze like a predator detects movement. "You said the devil would cease to exist," I said to her.

"Yes," she agreed, and it wasn't a lie. "That's why you have to surrender to him."

"They need you, Hennie!" Enon yelled over to me. "Because you are what's missing from them."

"In the original trinity, there is one God in three divine persons." Rachel's voice carried across the chasm of lava to me. I turned to look at her, ignoring the beast's insistence that I focus on my thoughts of death and destruction. "The Father is not the Son, the Son is not the Spirit, but all are God."

She said the words as if they were a revelation to her. As my frown deepened, her smile bloomed. Apparently, she had figured out Enon's stupid puzzle. "You are not the mind of the devil. You are not the anger of the devil." She smiled bigger, tears pouring from her eyes. "And you are not the body of the devil."

"But I am the devil?" I asked as much as said.

Rachel nodded slowly, losing some of her smile. "If you want to be."

I heard the words, and it nearly launched me into a new tirade. "Want to be? Who would ever want to be the devil? Who would choose to be something so heinous?"

"I would," Zeus said. I turned my attention to him.

My little coven had climbed onto the steps to save themselves from the lava that was oozing higher, threatening to overtake the bases of the surrounding buildings. Zeus was standing next to Enon, facing me. For a moment, he didn't speak. He just stared across a river of hell at the queen demon. I was certain his thoughts of a romance between us immediately evaporated in that moment.

Enon touched his arm, urging him to speak. Zeus took a breath, steeling himself for the words that were prematurely watering his eyes. "If you hurt enough. If the world hurts you enough. If you feel abandoned and alone. If you feel like everyone in your whole fucking life has never really loved you." He swallowed hard, pushing down the emotions that were breaking his voice. "That would make you choose to be something hideous and mean. That would make you want to hurt everyone around you, regardless of who they are. Because when it's all done... When everyone sees you for what you really are, their hatred can be justified. And then you can finally deserve the pain they caused you."

I stared at Zeus, unblinking. I had seen the similarities between my coven and myself. The trials I had endured were not unlike those of a ridiculed child. But until that moment, I hadn't realized how closely matched my pain was to Zeus's. His pain was so great that it had annihilated his goodwill and his survival instincts. At one time, he was willing to pick up a gun and kill simply to spread his pain onto others. He was ready to foster the horns of his own devilish image. All so he could look at himself in the mirror and have the strength to point that gun back at himself.

I knew that pain. Most of it was an old pain that I didn't fully understand, but it still hurt. It was a pain that didn't have an outlet. All I could do was let it build until it was ready to burst.

"It's you, Hennie," Dane said at my back. I whipped around to defend myself, but he wasn't attacking. He was standing on an upturned mound of earth. The same mound of earth I was now standing on. I glanced at the storefront on the edge of the street. The windows were still reflecting my image, but I was no longer wearing any extraneous limbs. There was, however, a tightly coiled snake wrapped around my neck. Just looking at it caused it to tighten.

I was overwhelmed by a lack of oxygen and the head rush that went with it.

"Hennie, no!" Dane rushed to my side. He was tugging on the snake with all of his might, but it wouldn't budge. Why was he even bothering to save me? He had tried to kill me more than once. Why not just let my shadow do it for him? "Stop! Stop it!" Dane shook me like an errant child.

"Jesus Christ, this is embarrassing," Enon said from behind me. I twisted to give him a glare, but he was burying his face in his hands and couldn't see my ire.

Was nothing serious to him? I was being strangled to death by the apple-dealer of Eden and all he could do was make fun of me. Maybe if he was so keen on keeping his power-mama, he should get off his ass and help me.

He looked up and met my furious gaze. The look on his face was the same as it always was when he thought I was being childish or ignorant or whatever. He raised his brow and shook his head like I should have put the puzzle together by now. "It's you, you simpleton. The serpent is you. You've been doing this all to yourself!"

My brow crumpled as a million thoughts passed by me. I couldn't grab onto any of them except the conversations I'd had with Dane and Jess.

It was my power that had created Dane. It gave him the ability to hunt and kill demons. It also gave him the ability to hunt me.

And as Jess said, I was part of the trinity, and yet all the things that had played out against me were from that trinity. She'd called it self-abuse.

Dane was above me now. I could feel the tight pressure on my neck and for a moment I thought he had taken over strangling me in place of the serpent. The tightly clenched teeth. The snarl. The dip in his brow making him look angry.

It wasn't anger, though. It was befuddlement. It was concentration and struggle and... fear.

He was trying to save me, but he couldn't.

Because I wouldn't let him.

I glanced over at the shop windows again. I was lying across the upheaved piece of street, turning blue from suffocation. This time I didn't see the winding, sinuous body of my serpent shadow around my neck. All I saw were my own hands.

Clamped around my neck, my fingers pressed hard enough to cut off my air supply. Hard enough to kill me. I was killing myself.

It no longer mattered if it was the serpent forcing my hands. I was him and he was me.

We were the same.

So, in the end, the diabolical scheming, the torment, the luring taste of hell's addictive power—I was, on some level, doing it all to *myself*.

CHAPTER 34

"Hennie, please," Dane petitioned me in a whisper. "Don't do this."

All at once, I realized he had never been the one trying to strangle me. I had been deluding myself into believing it was him, not willing to face the fact that I was doing it to myself. Why was this possible? I thought God didn't want the devil to die.

Not the devil. Me.

He didn't want me to die. He didn't want me to return to the trinity. He didn't want the devil's soul to remember. Why?

"Please, God," Dane finally said in exasperation. It was odd seeing him seek out God for help. He must have been desperate.

I could feel the connection to my coven still whispering to me. Tiny voices in the back of my mind. I relinquished the grip I had on my power. I allowed them the strength to assist me—to force my surrender.

I felt their hands on my legs and arms as if they were grabbing onto me and holding me down—much as they had in the merging ceremony. It was not the same connection I had with my sisters. The nature of our link was no doubt tainted by the method of its creation. In time, it would change, but for now, I would have to ignore the feeling of captivity that this union brought.

Though I had surrendered to my coven, the beast was not as easily swayed. It had only one desire, and that was for freedom and chaos. Claws ripped at my back, no longer trying to puppeteer me, but rather trying to rip through me. I wasn't sure it was possible, but if it could push past my very soul and take over the power, then all would be lost. A new devil would be born, worse than the last.

Enon finally joined the fight. The power ebbing from my soul was souring with the dark tang of hell. It was the perfect flavor for a hungry risen.

Enon drew in the darkness like a long drink. The beast recoiled from me. I still wasn't sure Enon could literally eat an incarnation of emotion, but he could obviously tame it.

Two greedy hands replaced one set of clawed paws. Much like the rest of my coven, I felt Enon's energy and mind pressing on me—containing me. I didn't like it. I didn't like how it felt to be subjugated, but at the moment, it was necessary.

When I still didn't let go of my throat, Enon drew on my power and narrowed his gaze at me. "Release," he commanded, and I did.

Dane gave him a wary look before pulling me up into his arms. He patted my back while I coughed. Even when I was through, he didn't release his embrace. I didn't fight it either. He wasn't trying to kill me. That revelation was enough to warrant a hug.

"Oh, bravo." Paula clapped her hands and shifted to a higher position on her rock. "This still doesn't change anything. You still can't stay here."

My ears perked up and for the first time in a long time, a sliver of hope trickled into my heart. I pushed away from Dane and frowned at Paula. "I heard that." I stood up and dusted myself off before facing her again. "That was a lie."

Paula raised her hands in surrender. "Oh, I'm sorry, let me clarify. If you stay here, then this big hellish hole you just created will continue to grow and grow until it swallows the Earth."

"You mean until God intervenes and closes it up, don't you?" I asked, jumping to the next island of street to get a better view of her.

"If he steps in, we will lose everything," Paula said.

"No." Rachel appeared out of nowhere on the rock next to mine. The other members of her coven, including Dane, materialized on the surrounding landmasses—creating a makeshift circle around Paula. I seriously needed to get my teleporting figured out. "The *we* she's referring to is *them*." Rachel turned to me. "You can stay, Hennie. I finally understand. I'm sorry it took me so long."

I looked between Paula's shaking head and Rachel's expectant eyes. "How?"

"The risen is right. You don't need them."

"Shut up!" Paula's body ripped away and a true devil rose in her place, a fiery body with sharp horns and cloven feet. "You are nothing without us!" she roared. She reached out to me, extending her growing reach. I leaped to Rachel's rock for safety. Meanwhile, my island broke apart, the bits quickly dissolving into the lava.

Rachel helped me up and linked her hand in mine. I looked down at the strange, friendly contact. "It's all lies." She brushed a piece of my hair from my face and

I was justly taken aback. I didn't know how to take this rekindled niceness—especially since she had never been this nice when we were friends. She smiled at me and I remembered the last time she had been this nice to me. In the basement, after I'd almost killed myself. She had been smiling and glowing, just like she was now. I looked back at the heavenly glow around her now. Was it this Rachel that had spoken to me that night? Was it this future version that sent a message back in time to me? Could she do that?

My attention moved back to the sisters who were lassoing the devil with white tendrils like cowboys rustling a calf. The devil was roaring and cutting each rope as quickly as it landed. Then a new set of ropes arrived. Long light blue cords wrapped around the devil's neck and feet. My new coven was joining the battle. Enon started moving the earth like chess pieces on a game board. The sisters danced in and out of each other's tethers as they passed by. My misfits jumped and weaved as well, avoiding getting beheaded by the power stretching across the chasm between them and the devil. They were tying the monster up. Tangling him in a web of power.

Rachel's and mine.

"Do you understand now?" Rachel asked.

I looked at her and I felt every bit the two years old that Enon claimed I was. I blinked stupidly at her, but she didn't laugh or mock me. She just smiled tenderly.

"You are the soul of the devil, Hennie. You are the first soul to ever be created. You are right here." Rachel poked my chest. "In your very own body, with your very own mind. Those thoughts and emotions you feel are all you. You are the devil, but you are not his rage." Rachel pointed to the fury displayed in the creature before me as he fell against the rubble he was standing on. I shielded myself from a spray of sparks that shot out when he hit. Rachel held out her hand, putting up an invisible barrier that blocked the twinkling embers. "And right now, you do not possess the devil's memories."

"They want me to remember," I said, trying to convince her I had followed along with some of Enon's puzzle.

"Yes, because when you remember who you are, when you remember your past, all that rage comes with it. If you choose to remember, then your soul and your mind become one. The first leg of hell's trinity. The memories will fuel the beast and the fires of hell will continue to burn inside of you."

I shook my head. "Why would I want that? Why have I... The serpent? He's been drawing me in. My own mind has been trying to put me back in that torment."

"I know."

"But why would I do that to myself?"

"Because you don't believe you deserve any better." I glanced over at the devil writhing and frothing as the covens pulled his ropes tighter and tighter. Shrinking him, as if the air was being let out of him. "You do." Rachel pulled my face back to look at me. "You do deserve to be loved." She was saying it so firmly it didn't feel like an affirmation, but more like a rebuke.

"How do we stop the apocalypse, though?"

"Just let go of your grip on your past life. Let go of the memories. Let go of the beast."

I looked over at Paula lying on the ground, tied up at every angle with ropes of power. Her devilish form diminished, sapped away along with her strength. She looked tired and old—no longer the beauty I knew her to be.

I could feel her now. A strange out-of-body experience, not unlike the one I'd experienced during my third exorcism.

Before I even realized it, I had teleported to her rock. I tip-toed through the veins of power that were containing her and stopped near her head. She looked up at me—a seething mass of contempt. Despite the rage of the beast being inside of me, her link to it was still strong. The memories of past wrongs were fresh in her mind. She labored against them every day. Even with her time as a human, she hadn't softened. She may have enjoyed being here as a human, but her mind remained entrenched in hell. Her plots and schemes were all that kept her content enough to carry on.

I kneeled down next to her. "What happens when I lose my memories completely?"

"The devil will cease to exist," she answered.

I noted the specificity of her answer. Not die. Just... cease to exist. And not me. Not this body. I would still live on.

Was that okay? Would He allow that?

A thought occurred to me, and I looked at Enon. He raised a brow, ready for the Q&A. "You said some apocalypses were caused by humans. Meaning that most of them weren't."

Enon nodded. "Yeah."

"What caused the majority of them?" I asked.

He took a breath and shook his head. "Don't ask questions you don't want the answers to."

"Who caused the majority of them?" I clarified.

Paula laughed at my feet, but I ignored her and waited for Enon's answer. He rolled his jaw and looked at me through lazy half-lidded eyes. "You did."

I looked down at Paula. "How many times have I run away? How many times have I left hell and taken a human form?"

She smirked at me. "Hundreds. Thousands. What does it matter?"

I took a breath, trying to imagine running away from myself thousands of times. How many bodies had I inhabited against their will? How many times had I tasted a human existence only to fall back down to hell again? Like Sisyphus, I was reliving my fall from heaven over and over again, the only way I knew how.

"You always come back to us," Paula's voice rasped as three overlapping tones came out. The woman, the man, and the beast. I swallowed, staring into her horizontal pupils. She was the only future I had to look forward to. I would be foolish to think this time would end any differently than the others. It was all for naught.

"Wait!" Rachel was suddenly beside me. I looked at her and she nodded to Paula. "Ask her how many times God has sanctified your soul?"

I turned back to Paula. Her jaw was rolling like she was chewing cud. "How many?" I asked.

I could tell she didn't want to answer, but she was compelled to. "Once."

I glanced at Rachel and saw her pinch back a smile. "How many times have I been the only soul in a living human body?" I asked.

"Once."

I huffed out a sigh of relief and allowed myself to relax. Maybe this time really was different. Maybe this was possible. Maybe the devil could forget and move on. "What happens to hell if the devil ceases to exist?"

"Oh, don't worry about that." Enon appeared on our island and stepped over a few power lines to get closer to me. "There are plenty of demons to keep it running." He pulled a knife from his back pocket and handed it to me.

I stared at it, confused. "What is this for?"

"I told you we wouldn't get out of this without someone dying." Enon nodded to Paula.

I looked at the knife and at her. I knew it was technically my body, and that Paula was a branch of me, but it still felt more like homicide than suicide to kill her.

But Enon was right. I needed to dissolve the trinity once and for all. Otherwise, I was just going to be pushing another rock up another hill.

I looked at Rachel. She frowned at me, but nodded. She understood what needed to be done. Killing my human body would return my soul to the trinity. But killing my original body would make all three cease to exist.

I raised the blade over Paula, but stopped. I drew it back again. There seemed to be a collective gasp as if everyone was afraid I was going to go back on my decision and transform into a hell's angel again.

I looked over to Dane, and he dipped his brow, asking without words what was wrong.

I looked down at the knife in my hand before giving it back to Enon. "I won't need that."

He gave me a questioning look, but put the knife away.

Instead of using the blade, I reached out for my power. There was some resistance on the strength, as if everyone was a bit touchy about giving me the reins, but I sensed Enon release his grip in a generous offering of trust. I focused on my task to get it just right. Then I opened my mouth and spoke the actuating word.

"Forget."

Paula's face wrenched in horror. "No!" she screamed, just as her body turned to ash. The voice of my shadow's identical objection resonated in my mind for a moment longer, but it too faded away. All that remained was a lump of clothing tangled in magical ropes. Everyone relaxed their hold on their offenses, letting the tethers evaporate.

I looked at Rachel to see if I had really done it. She smiled at me.

There was a belated relief that settled into the group. My coven started climbing over the now chilly street rubble to high-five each other and revel in their first brush with death. My former coven hugged each other and wept—relieved to be done with the war.

I was relieved as well. Paula was gone. My shadow was gone.

I could still feel my power, but it was only mine. There was nothing from hell, apart from whatever Enon brought to our coven. I turned to Rachel to thank her for her help, but she pulled me into a hug before I could speak. I leaned into her, enjoying the good juju that ebbed off her like a sweet perfume.

I was free.

CHAPTER 35

T HE BAR BEING FILLED with nuns was putting more than a few of the locals on edge, but they soon figured out that only a few of them were proper nuns. I wasn't sure when Meredith started dancing a jig on the bar, but someone pulled out an accordion and played for her. The barflies clapped along. Everyone erupted when she pulled up her robe to show off her legs.

Zeus, Puck, and Vlad were having a heyday retelling their day to each other. Raven was sitting with them, but she wasn't taking part in the conversation so much as watching Enon. He had opted to sit at my table. As if it wasn't odd enough being in a room with my former and current coven post-almost-apocalypse, I was being subjected to the discomfort of sitting at a table with my former frenemy, ex-boyfriend, and ex-ex-boyfriend.

I glanced over at Rachel on my right and gave her a small smile. "It's good to see that Meredith is as extroverted as ever."

She smiled—though it was a strained smile. Her benevolence had worn off at some point and her more rigid humanity was poking through her facade. I knew she wasn't really sitting with me so much as babysitting me. I think somewhere in the back of her mind, she suspected this was a trick. She was already a suspicious person, but Paula had made her paranoid. I couldn't blame her, but it made me feel a little like a petri dish.

"So, this is the ex?" Enon observed, making the already awkward moment worse.

I glanced across the table at Dane. He had been watching me, but I couldn't look at him. Everything was very complicated now. I knew it wasn't Dane that had been trying to kill me, but it had ultimately been their plan to remove me, which would have killed this body anyway, and put me back in hell. It didn't matter, I suppose, since they'd thought they were doing the right thing. None of us had known there was another option.

However, it wasn't my disapproval of his hunting that had my head sagging. It was my shame. I had cheated on him. Again, I was pretty sure we were over the minute his sexual intentions became predatory, but now, with all that in the past, I was stuck with a dirt-bag fling I couldn't get rid of. I glanced at Enon, giving him a glare that begged him to shut up.

"Does that make you Hennie's current boyfriend?" Rachel asked casually before taking a sip of the beer Enon had graciously bought everyone.

Enon smirked at me and looked over the glare I was still holding for him. "No, I don't think so. My charm tends to wear off pretty fast. Plus, Hennie isn't nearly as appealing to me without that beautiful rage inside of her."

"So you were only in it for my mind after all," I mumbled.

Enon chuckled and glanced over at Raven, who nodded toward the exit. He smirked at her and gave a small nod before holding up his finger for her to wait. "If you're feeling slighted, there's always room for another devotee."

I looked over at Raven as she fiddled with her hair, eagerly anticipating Enon's exit. Even after she found out he was a demon, she didn't care. She truly was a desperate girl. I wondered if she knew Enon had other covens, as Zeus had said. Perhaps that was why she was fighting so hard to keep his attention—too much competition to demand monogamy.

"Take it easy on her, would you?" I said rather than rise to his bait. "Unlike you, she actually has a heart."

"You don't give her enough credit. Unlike some women, Raven knows I'm worth waiting in line for."

"Eww!" I leaned back in my chair, instantly regretting every encounter I had shared with him.

"So, if you aren't interested in Hennie anymore," Rachel said, disrupting our bickering, "perhaps we should get her reconnected with her sisters instead—excuse me, and brother," she added, nodding to Dane.

Dane and I exchanged a horrified look.

"Please don't refer to me as her brother," Dane said.

"I just mean you don't have to run anymore, Hennie. You can come home. If you want." Rachel's smile was still tense, as if she were begging me to comply, rather than demanding, as she wanted to. I suspected what she was offering was more like house arrest.

"Oh, I don't think so. Hennie is still a very powerful being. Just because she isn't ignited by her wrath anymore doesn't mean I don't want her." Enon leaned over and squeezed my leg under the table. I shifted away, but he kept hold of me. "I know what you're all thinking."

"I'm not sure you do," Dane said. "Because you're still sitting here." I felt a warble of magic come off him that exuded power. I glanced at Rachel, but she didn't seem to disapprove of Dane flexing his muscles with her source. In fact, she seemed to be just fine with it. I wondered if this was more what Sister Aggie had in mind for Dane when she'd suggested his forced contrition.

Enon smiled at Dane. "Oh, I like you. I've met one like you before, but I'm always happy to know another." Enon released my leg and focused his attention on Rachel. "You're already plotting how to get rid of me. How to disconnect her from me."

Rachel smiled at him—it was genuine, which was weird. "You're very intuitive, risen."

"Well, don't bother, you can't." The words rang with falsehood, but I didn't call Enon out on it.

"I think you're underestimating us, risen," Rachel said.

"And you're underestimating me. You're both being foolish. You're tied up in your morality and he's tied up in his cock." Enon nodded to each of them. "In case you didn't notice, Hennie is not designed for this world. I'm the only thing strong enough to anchor her, should she decide to flip her switch again." Enon stood up to leave. He looked me over, contemplating his words. He bit his lip before turning to Dane. "Take her if you want. It makes no difference if she's here or there. I will have access to her power, no matter the distance."

"For now," Dane said.

Enon looked him over, but allowed him to get the last word in. He moved to the bar and threw a pinch of hundred-dollar bills down for the bartender. His tip for the night. He barely had time to get to the door before Raven was on his heels.

"Why do I get the feeling that man is going to be more of a nuisance than a help?" Rachel said before drinking down a gulp of her beer.

I was about to mention he had lied about us not being able to remove him, but Dane abruptly pushed his chair back and stood. "Can I speak to you, Hennie? Alone?"

I looked up at the stern expression on his face. This would not be a fun conversation. I glanced at Rachel and she gave me a piteous look. As soon as I pushed myself away from the table, Dane stomped off into the hall outside the door.

I groaned and took a swig of my beer. After a few steps, I came back to the table. "Did you really mean what you said about me joining the coven again, or are you just trying to get me away from Enon?"

Rachel shifted under my gaze. "I wish you wouldn't ask questions that will inevitably catch me in a lie." She took a breath and held it for a moment as she considered how to answer. "All I can say... is I very much want to want you back. We have a long road ahead of us. I have a lot of questions that need to be answered."

"Like what?"

"Nothing that needs to be answered *right now*. Go. Talk to Dane. I don't think he can hold that portal open for much longer." Rachel nodded to where Dane had been standing at the door. There was a flickering image behind him.

I scoffed. "Seriously? You guys are so much cooler than me. If I come home, you'll teach me how to do that stuff, right?"

Rachel smirked at me. "We'll see," she said, back to her benevolent self. It wasn't a yes, but it was the best I could hope for until she trusted me more.

I headed over to Dane and paused at the opening of his portal. I glanced at the table of misfits who were observing me. I suspected they sensed my dread and were watching to see if I needed help. Before leaving, I showed them my most exaggerated and comical grimace to let them know I was okay, just suffering a bit of social anxiety.

Stepping through the portal, I found myself in my parents' living room. Dane came through after me and bumped into me, forcing me to move further into the room. I watched him release the portal with a flourish of his fingers. The opening shriveled into nothingness. "Since when did you get so good at magic?" I asked, unable to hide my envy.

"As Rachel would say, power is not a skill."

"Mmm, I guess I missed the sensei portion of the coven sisterhood."

"Yes, you missed a lot of things."

"Yeah, I guess." I crossed my arms and leaned on the couch. He was at the other end, standing tall and proud, like at any minute he might draw a weapon. "How did that conversation go? Did Rachel get down on one knee before proposing you join the coven?"

"Actually, I was the one on my knees." I frowned and waited for him to explain. "When I sensed whatever was inside of you, I knew something was wrong. It wasn't until your charm blocked me that I truly realized my intentions were not good." Dane sat down on the arm of the couch. "The more intense my desire became, the more I realized I couldn't fight it forever. That's when I petitioned Rachel... to kill me."

My shoulders sagged. "Kill you?"

"It was the only way to protect you. I tried to do it myself, but I couldn't. Whatever you had done to me made me incapable of harming myself."

"So, she opted to make you part of the coven."

"I don't think she wanted to, but since she couldn't remove my cravings without disrupting my ability to track you, she opted for a merge. The veil of magic brought me a lot a clarity." Dane looked at the floor. "I think I belong with them. More than I did before."

I tried not to be envious, but I couldn't muster the strength to fake it. "That's great. I'm so happy you could be a part of something so spectacular. I'm sorry I missed your transition into a super-hot warlock, but I was working in the food industry, begging for tips to feed myself."

Dane stared at me, his jaw clenching. "Are we really going to compare infidelities right now?"

I looked down and kicked the corner of the couch. "No."

"Is what he said true? Is it over between you two?"

I nodded and pulled back my collar to show where the brand had healed and disappeared. "I still share a connection to him through the coven, but it's not nearly as strong."

"I guess that will have to do for now."

"Where does that leave us?"

Dane pinned me with a treacherous look. "Where do you want that to leave us?" he asked.

I rubbed my arms, suddenly feeling the cold. "Rachel wants me back here. I think she wants to keep an eye on me. I don't know if she's ever going to trust me again, but I'm going to do my best to stay on her good side."

"That's where you're at with Rachel. What about us?"

"I'm asking you that."

"And I'm asking you."

"I don't get to decide, Dane. I'm the cheater, remember? That means I have to worm my way back into your life."

"Do you want to be back in my life?"

"Yes."

"Why?" he asked flatly.

"What do you mean, *why*?"

"Why do you want to be in my life?" Dane clarified.

"Because… Because I love you." My volume trailed off as I realized how ridiculous I sounded.

Dane stood and moved to me. "There. That's what I wanted to hear you say." He caressed my cheek, and I closed my eyes and leaned into it. I hadn't stopped thinking about Dane since I left. Standing before him made me feel weak and vulnerable. I wanted to beg and plead for forgiveness, but I was afraid to. I was afraid he would refuse me and reject me.

I felt his lips hit my neck, and I gasped. "Aren't you going to yell at me or something?"

"No," he whispered in my ear before unbuttoning my pants. "We've spent enough time punishing each other. I want to welcome you home." He pulled my shirt off over my head and paused as he looked at the spot where my brand used to be. I thought perhaps it was going to ruin the mood, but he just smirked and grabbed my hand. "Come on, I don't think you'll mind that I'm a warlock when you see what I can do for you." Dane tugged me along. He led me up the stairs and into the bedroom, where he made me forget all about my former addictions, including my bond with Enon and the draw of the devil. My only addiction would now be to Dane, but I could finally call it love.

CHAPTER 36

I WOKE FROM A nightmare about fire and brimstone. I looked to Dane slumbering beside me. Our lovemaking had put him out like a light. He was oblivious to my fitful sleeping.

I moved to crawl back into his warm embrace when I noticed the smell of smoke had not stopped at my nightmare. Concerned for the safety of my house, as well as any number of supernatural concerns—including Paula rising from the ashes of her death—I ran out of the room in search of the fire.

I tapped into my magic to get a better nose and sniffed my way to the kitchen. I ran in, ready to put out a grease fire, but there were no flames in sight.

The room was quiet and dark. I caught movement out of the corner of my eye and turned to face the figure in the shadows.

Turned away from me, sitting at my breakfast table smoking a cigarette, was Sister Aggie.

My heart flipped and sank at once. I was happy to see her, and yet seeing her meant something different from seeing Jess.

"Sit down," she ordered in no uncertain terms.

I was in grade school again, being scolded by her. I didn't bother to go through any list of questions I had. I just sat down in the chair catty-corner to her and waited for my homework assignment.

Sister Aggie sat there staring out at my backyard, smoking her cigarette for nearly a minute before she spoke. "Do you have any idea of the sacrifice that has been made for you?"

I blinked, not quite sure whether this was a question I was supposed to agree to on principle or whether there really was a definitive definition I needed to be aware of.

"The devil—on Earth. It's unheard of." Sister Aggie finally looked at me and I wished she hadn't. She wasn't mad, per se, but so very stern. So very grave in her assertions. "It's never happened before, Hennie. Not like this. Not with His permission."

I gulped, realizing this wasn't so much a scolding from Sister Aggie as a message from... Dad.

"Do you think you deserve this opportunity?" she was asking, but again, I wasn't sure I should answer. "It's not you, you know?" She stared at me, now looking more perturbed. "It's your mother, your father, Jess, me. We all gave you the tools necessary to be a good person."

I nodded. That, at least, I knew.

"So don't think for one second you did anything to earn the right to be on this Earth."

Tears stung my eyes. I was feeling every bit of this lecture like a child discovering that disappointment was worse than anger and expectations were harder to live up to than goals.

Sister Aggie shook her head and continued to smoke her cigarette for a while. "We'll try this once, but if you screw it up, He won't let you do it again."

"I won't screw it up, I promise."

"Don't make promises you have no control over."

"I'll only use my power for good." Sister Aggie threw me a look of disdain. "Or not at all, if that's what you want."

"Rachel will continue to guide you. She's spent a lot of time learning to harness her own demons. You'll do fine with her as an instructor."

I felt relieved knowing Rachel would eventually forgive me and teach me how I wanted.

"But in the end, it will still be up to you," Aggie said rather dismally. "You will have to decide who you want to be. Hennie or the devil."

"I've already decided. I made myself forget. The ram is gone. The serpent is gone. The beast is gone." Even as I said the words, I heard a low growl behind me. I instinctively looked back, but saw nothing in the kitchen space. I turned to the window where I could see a vague reflection of something in the far corner near the island. Dark skin creased with just a hint of smoldering red. The twitching tail sent chills down my spine. "No. No. I forgot my memories. My mind is gone. The beast should be gone."

"It's not that simple."

I turned to Sister Aggie, my eyes pleading. "Make it go away. Tell Him to make it go away."

"I can't. He can't. That..." Aggie tossed her finger back toward the low rumble somewhere behind her. "Is as much a part of your soul as it was a part of your mind. You can forget who you are, but you will still carry with you that great capacity for rage."

"Does that mean...?"

"Yes, you are still a very dangerous presence on this Earth. If you do not contain your rage, you will cause another apocalypse. And if that happens..."

"I go back to hell," I finished. I was starting to understand why Enon had suggested I needed him. He was the only one that could stop me if I had another... episode.

"No." Sister Aggie crushed out her cigarette on a plate and stood. "I'm afraid not, Hennie." She moved to my side and stroked my head, pushing my hair behind my ear. "This is the devil's last chance." She frowned at me. "If this doesn't work, then He will take back your soul."

"He'll kill me?" I asked.

Sister Aggie nodded and squeezed my shoulder. "But don't worry. You still have a chance to redeem yourself in His eyes. All you need to do is prove that you can surmount your humanity and..."

"Not start an apocalypse?"

"Exactly." Sister Aggie moved to the kitchen entrance as if she planned on leaving by the front door rather than an ethereal gateway. She turned back and smiled at me. "I have every faith that you can do this, Hennie."

She disappeared into the hall and I took in a soothing breath. It was a lot of pressure to be the one responsible for redeeming or damning the devil. I wished I could say I agreed with Sister Aggie about my ability to keep the beast extinguished, but since her last statement had been a lie, I guess neither one of us really had faith in me.

FELICIA JEDLICKA

The
Necromancer's
Child

The Necromancer's Child

"Miracle Girl Survives Deadly Fire"

That was just one of the many headlines circulating after Tori Blake was pulled from the burnt wreckage of a car fire that killed her parents. Without so much as a scratch on her, no one could explain how she survived such a horrific disaster while her parents incinerated.

Traumatized by the event, Tori's childhood memories were extinguished, along with the flames. With only vague recollections of happy times and parental love, she returns home fourteen years later to uncover the truth about her parents' deaths.

Unanswered questions about the fire's combustion and its intensity have fueled the rumor mill in Harold. Though she initially dismisses the whispers about witchcraft and devil worship, Tori finds it harder to disregard the possibility of a paranormal cause after she discovers her home is being haunted by its former residents.

The deeper she digs into the past, the more tarnished her image of her perfect family becomes. With her investigation soured by accounts of abuses and betrayals, Tori embraces her inherited mantle of necromancy and starts interrogating the dead.

A dark stranger from her parent's past resurfaces to continue his torment. Tori must find a way to push this renegade ghost back into the spirit world or suffer the same fate as her parents.

Thank you so much for reading. I hope you
enjoyed the ride and if you aren't getting
off here, I encourage you to sign up for my
newsletter so I can return your generosity
with new release updates and special offers.

Sign-Up

You can also find me on Facebook or visit my
website. Keep reading!

Website

Facebook

About the Author

As a Nebraska native, and a small-town girl at that, I have very little to occupy my time beyond imagining a world outside of my own reality. By the grace of God and the seat of my pants, I have kept my waning attention span on the task of becoming an author.

So here I am, an indie author, peddling my words in cyberspace and enduring my comeuppances with an unwavering determination. I may not be a professional, and I certainly am not perfect, but if you've made it this far, you have to admit, this smartass yokel does spin quite a yarn.

From the self-inflicted sweatshop conditions of my unairconditioned childhood home, to the arthritis reaping positions of a sedentary lifestyle, I bring to you: my sarcasm, my oddity, and my heart. Take it with a grain of salt or a teaspoon of sugar, but take it for what it is: a story born of the mind, translated to paper, and gifted to you.

I thank you for your readership and even more for your support. Please recommend this book to your friends and family via any social media that you use. Word of mouth is still the best advertising and is greatly appreciated.

Most importantly, keep reading. I'll keep writing.